"I've never had a day like this," she said. "Best of times and worst of times."

"Yeah? What was the best?" In his mind, he replayed their kiss by Teacup Lake.

"The autopsy, of course."

He should have guessed. "And the worst?"

"Being scared by the big bad Wolff."

He appreciated her sense of humor but knew she used jokes to deflect her real feelings. This woman didn't like being vulnerable. "I'm sorry that happened to you. If I'd been with you, Wolff never would have come close."

"True. You're definitely an alpha male."

"Can we be serious for a minute? I'd feel better if I could—with your permission—keep an eye on you."

"Like a bodyguard?"

Exactly like a bodyguard.

SHALLOW GRAVE

USA TODAY Bestselling Author
CASSIE MILES

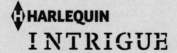

HARLEQUIN
INTRIGUE

To my New York family: Signe, Aaron and Finn. Can't wait to see you all. And, as always, to Rick.

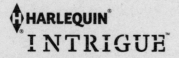

HARLEQUIN®
INTRIGUE™

Recycling programs for this product may not exist in your area.

ISBN-13: 978-1-335-58245-4

Shallow Grave

Copyright © 2023 by Kay Bergstrom

For questions and comments about the quality of this book, please contact us at CustomerService@Harlequin.com.

Harlequin Enterprises ULC
22 Adelaide St. West, 41st Floor
Toronto, Ontario M5H 4E3, Canada
www.Harlequin.com

Printed in U.S.A.

Cassie Miles, a *USA TODAY* bestselling author, lived in Colorado for many years and has now moved to Oregon. Her home is an hour from the rugged Pacific Ocean and an hour from the Cascade Mountains—the best of both worlds—not to mention the incredible restaurants in Portland and award-winning wineries in the Willamette Valley. She's looking forward to exploring the Pacific Northwest and finding mysterious new settings for Harlequin Intrigue romances.

Books by Cassie Miles

Harlequin Intrigue

Mountain Retreat
Colorado Wildfire
Mountain Bodyguard
Mountain Shelter
Mountain Blizzard
Frozen Memories
The Girl Who Wouldn't Stay Dead
The Girl Who Couldn't Forget
The Final Secret
Witness on the Run
Cold Case Colorado
Find Me
Gaslighted in Colorado
Escape from Ice Mountain
Shallow Grave

Visit the Author Profile page at Harlequin.com.

CAST OF CHARACTERS

Daisy Brighton—While the high school anatomy teacher from Denver researches hidden outlaw treasure in mountain graveyards, she discovers evidence of a serial killer.

A. P. Carter—A National Park Service (NPS) ranger and investigator, he tracks down the killer using his knowledge and love of the mountains.

Violet Rhodes (Aunt Vi)—Daisy's vivacious sixty-eight-year-old aunt, who lives in Leadville.

The Good Guys—FBI agents Pat Wiley and Mickey Hicks, medical examiner Dr. Julia Sweetwater, and NPS director Joaquin Stanley.

Suspects—Jackknife Jones, Slade Franklin, and Eric and Gerald Wolff.

Victims—Rene Williams, Andrea Lindstrom, Hannah Guerrero and Eileen Findlay.

Chapter One

"Are we lost?"

"Not hardly." Jackknife Jones stuck his head out the window of his ramshackle truck and spat tobacco juice onto the two-lane gravel road. "Don't you worry your purty little head. I'll get you where you're going."

Daisy Brighton turned her head—which really wasn't all that purty or little—away from the grizzled old man behind the steering wheel and stared impatiently through the filthy windshield. Over an hour and a half ago when they'd left her aunt Violet Rhodes's house in Leadville, sunset had painted the skies above the Saguache Range in shades of magenta streaked by golden clouds and framed by blue spires of ponderosa pine and spruce. A snowy-white cloak draped over Mount Elbert, even though it was mid-June.

She'd expected to reach the cemetery before nightfall. *No such luck.* Obviously, Jackknife had no idea where he was going. Jostling on unpaved roads, the truck meandered and doubled back and circled around. Dusk had settled. Daisy was furious.

The headlight beam splashed across a boulder where someone had scrawled a heart and initials: RAH + KB.

She scowled. "Mr. Jones, I'm sure we already passed that graffiti."

"Like I told you, call me Jackknife." He cackled. "Don't let my name scare you."

It took more than a jackknife to frighten Daisy. For the past seven years, she'd taught high school biology in Denver, and a classroom full of teenagers was enough to strike terror into just about anybody, especially when she handed out scalpels for frog dissections.

Jackknife swerved the truck into an almost invisible right turn, and they continued to weave through San Isabel National Park and private property that was fenced off with barbed wire. They hadn't passed a town for miles.

She looked down at her cell phone. No bars. The GPS had quit working. No maps available. "You said the cemetery is near Butcher's Gulch, correct?"

"It's called a boot hill, sweet thang. Criminals and poor folks got buried there. Being left in a boot hill usually meant a violent death. These souls got kilt so fast they died with their boots on."

His description seemed apt for what she'd discovered from research into her ancestors—a motley collection of scoundrels, cheats, gunslingers and bandits. Her project over the summer break was to track down the final resting place for Sherwood Brighton, an outlaw who died in 1896. Her aunt believed her great-great-great-grandfather's grave would lead to the hiding place of his ill-gotten gains and had recruited Daisy to search. Already, she'd visited eight cemeteries.

"Just to be clear," she said. "You told Aunt Vi that you saw a grave marker in this boot hill cemetery with the name Brighton on it."

"You betcha." He tucked a fresh chaw of tobacco into his cheek. *Disgusting habit.* "Lemme ask you something about your auntie. Is she seeing anybody?"

"You mean dating?"

"I sure as heck do. Vi is a fine-looking woman."

Daisy wouldn't argue with that. Her aunt was tall and maintained her slim figure with daily exercise at the Leadville Yoga Center. The sun-streaked blond of her chin-length bob was dyed to match the color of Daisy's ponytail, and they both had green eyes. Vi was definitely stylish. Also, she was sixty-eight years old. Not that her age meant she couldn't have a boyfriend or two. But Daisy couldn't help feeling a twinge of irritation when she realized that Jackknife wanted her to play matchmaker. When was the last time a man had shown interest in Daisy? Here she sat on a Saturday night—date night—in a junky truck with a creep who'd offered to show her a cemetery.

"Violet doesn't have a steady guy," she muttered.

"Mebbe you could put in a good word for me."

Not going to happen. Her lips pinched together, holding back the obvious truth. No way would classy Vi go out with Jackknife unless he made some changes, starting with giving up tobacco. Also, he needed to shave the patchy whiskers. And it wouldn't hurt if he changed clothes and took a long, hot bath in industrial-strength disinfectant.

Still, she didn't want to alienate her ride home. Grudgingly, she said, "Maybe."

"Your auntie owns her house, right? She oughta have a man around to take care of her."

"Doesn't need a bodyguard. She's got a double-barreled shotgun."

"Does she have any other property? What about money in the bank?"

She gaped. Was this backwoods gigolo going after Vi for her money? Before she could tell him to back off, Daisy heard the discordant echo of electronic music. *In the middle of the forest?* The headlights shone on a sign for Butcher's Gulch Campground. "Finally! We're here."

"Nope, not yet," he said. "The ghost town is a coupla miles more, and then—"

"Stop. Right now." In a teacher voice that didn't allow for discussion, she gave the orders. "You're going to drive into the campground, where I can ask for directions."

Grumbling, he parked beside the Butcher's Gulch sign. "You shouldn't get out of the truck. Ain't safe."

"I can handle some kids playing their music too loud." As if to emphasize her point, the volume lowered. "See. Not dangerous."

"The boot hill's haunted," he said. "And there's rumors of a man beast in a ski mask who attacks purty young girls like you."

Not wanting to argue until she got safely back to Leadville, she said nothing but got out of the truck, put on a denim jacket over her red cotton shirt and followed the gravel road that looped through a small campground. The two slots nearest the entrance provided parking for several vehicles, ranging from trucks and SUVs to a racy little sports car. She counted four tents and more than a dozen college-age people gathered around two fire pits. Some of them continued to dance to the tamped-down music while others guzzled beer from red plastic cups.

Asking the partygoers for directions seemed like a

waste of time. This crew would be lucky to find their way to the outhouse in the middle of the night. She almost pivoted and returned to Jackknife's truck when she noticed a gunmetal-gray SUV with a National Park Service shield on the door. The tall man who reached for the door handle on the driver's side didn't wear the typical flat-brimmed hat, but he had a bison badge pinned to his dark green vest. A park ranger. He was exactly what she needed.

She approached him. "Excuse me."

The reflected blaze from the campfire flared in his deep-set eyes and outlined the sharp edge of his jawbone, which contrasted with full, well-shaped lips. When he looked at her, he didn't smile, which was a bit disconcerting. "Can I help you?"

She met his unsmiling gaze with a toothy grin. "I'm looking for the Butcher's Gulch boot hill."

"Are you staying in this campground?"

"No."

"Coming to the party?" He gestured to the young people who barely looked old enough to drink but were carefully behaving within the limits of the law.

She widened her grin, probably causing him to wonder why she was so delighted to be searching for a cemetery. "You see, my ancestor is Sherwood Brighton, and I'm trying to find his grave. I'm Daisy Brighton."

He touched the brim of his weathered brown cowboy hat as he introduced himself. "I'm A. P. Carter. I go by Carter."

"Please call me Daisy." She nodded toward his badge. "You're a ranger."

"National Park Service, investigative services branch."

Finally, he smiled. "And you're the heir to the legendary Brighton's Bullion."

"I am." She nodded, not surprised he'd heard the story of hidden treasure.

A pink-haired woman in skimpy cutoffs and combat boots sashayed toward them. She batted her superlong eyelashes at Carter. "What legend? Please tell me, Mr. Ranger."

He lived up to Daisy's expectations of an honorable park ranger when he put distance between himself and Pinkie. Though too young for the ranger and too drunk, she was clearly smitten. And who could blame her? Carter was a good-looking guy with a great smile when he chose to use it. He gave Daisy a nod. "Go ahead, Ms. Brighton, tell the story."

"My ancestor, Sherwood Brighton, was an outlaw. In 1887, he pulled off a robbery on the Denver–Rio Grande Railroad." Pinkie had already lost interest and scooted closer to Carter, which annoyed Daisy. Though the NPS ranger might not actually be her Saturday-night date, he could have been. At least, she was age appropriate at twenty-nine. He couldn't be more than midthirties.

To get Pinkie's attention, she used a teacher trick, waving a shiny object at the student. "Do you know how much a kilobar of gold bullion is worth?"

"A what?" Pinkie asked.

"Kilobar. It's a brick, about two pounds of solid gold."

"How big?" Pinkie held out the hand that wasn't wrapped around a red plastic cup. "Could I hold it?"

"It's about the same size as a paperback book. One kilobar is worth about $56,000 at today's rates. Sherwood Brighton stole fifty of them. He got away, and the bullion was never found." The math, she suspected, would be beyond Pinkie. "Fifty kilobars at fifty-six thou each. That's $2.8 million."

"No way." Pinkie downed her beer with one glug, straightened her shoulders and motioned to the others. "Hey, we've got to look for the kilobars."

Carter leaned close and said, "Should I give her the bad news or will you?"

"Let me." Daisy waited until the dancers and drinkers gathered around. "Brighton's Bullion has been missing since 1887. Hundreds have searched. No one has found it." Which was why she had no problem telling the story.

"I wish you luck on the search." Carter stepped forward and addressed the party-goers. "In the meantime, you people need to keep the music low, watch your fires and don't drive drunk. If I get another complaint about disorderly conduct and have to come here again, tickets will be issued and some of you will be taken into custody."

When they started to complain, he slashed his hand and cut off their voices. "That's final."

"Excuse me," Daisy said. "Directions to the boot hill?"

He took her arm, escorted her to the passenger side of his vehicle and opened the door. "Might be easier if I take you there."

She was about to regretfully refuse when she glanced toward the entry sign. The truck was gone. Jackknife had dumped her without transportation in the middle of San Isabel National Park. Though justifiably ticked off, she wouldn't complain. The old tobacco chewer's indifference resulted in her riding with Ranger A. P.

Carter, which had to be pure serendipity. Cheerfully, she climbed into his SUV.

"Where did you park your vehicle?" he asked.

"At my aunt's house where I'm staying in Leadville."

"You're a long way from home." His smile dissolved, and he regarded her with the same kind of authoritative hostility that had silenced the pesky campers. "How did you get here?"

"I caught a ride with a friend of my aunt. We got lost, and when I saw the sign for the campground, I wanted to stop and ask for directions. He must have taken off."

"Not much of a friend. Come with me."

Carter's SUV had been kept in tip-top condition, ensuring a smooth ride, a quiet engine and precisely controlled temperature, but she couldn't relax. Daisy didn't like his disapproving attitude. She wasn't a flake and had never been a troublemaker. The opposite, in fact—she was the sort of woman who solved problems and was prepared for crises. Even now, when she might have been helpless and stranded, she'd thought to bring her cell phone and had a wallet with twenty bucks and a credit card in her pocket. It might be too far to get back to Leadville tonight, but she could manage.

When he looked toward her, she studied his face in the glow from the dashboard. His eyes were bright blue, and his hair was black. His smile had disappeared. "You're not a happy camper."

"Don't worry, Ms. Brighton. I'll make sure you get home in one piece."

"Call me Daisy."

"Okay… Daisy. Now, what's the procedure when we get to the cemetery?"

"I find markers and read names. Some are carved in

stone. Others are faded scribbles on weathered wood. Many of the old cemeteries have undergone restoration, which means the graves are neatly outlined with stones and the inscriptions displayed clearly." The tombstones often left poignant epitaphs, such as "lynched and deserved it" or "trampled in stampede, died too young" or "stabbed by heartless wife."

"What led you here?" he asked. "What is it about this particular boot hill?"

"The guy who abandoned me said he saw a marker with Brighton written on it. Don't know if I can believe him, but it's worth a look."

Carter tapped the brake and brought the SUV to a near stop before bumping off the road and over the shoulder onto a track through high grasses and sagebrush. After about fifty yards, he parked and announced, "Welcome to Butcher's Gulch."

Before she left the SUV, he handed her an extra flashlight from the glove compartment. Outside, she noticed more of a chill in the air and fastened two buttons on her denim jacket. Her imagination cranked into high gear as she approached the ruins of the ghost town. The beam of her flashlight slid up and down a stone fireplace attached to a crumbling stone wall. A window without glass stood above the rickety planks of a porch. The ruins of what might have been a main street formed a line on one side. There was another fireplace. And a broken-down wagon with a busted wheel. A tire swing hung from a low tree branch.

Her gaze lifted, and she looked up at a million diamond-bright stars and a quarter moon. Whatever life energy populated Butcher's Gulch had scattered on the summer breeze and vanished in the pine-scented mountain air. She didn't believe in ghosts but felt the presence of memories. Long ago, these tumbledown houses had been filled with laughter and the sounds of children singing. Families had embraced. Lovers had kissed. But there had also been tears and tragedies. A shiver constricted the muscles in her neck. Had there been fear? Were there screams that slashed through the night?

WALKING SLOWLY AND enjoying the cool summer night, Carter came up beside Daisy. When he touched her shoulder, she reacted with a shiver. Her face tilted up toward his, and her gaze flickered as though afraid to settle too long and become trapped.

"Something wrong?" he asked.

"I had an illogical premonition of danger."

"Not so odd. We're on our way to a boot hill."

"But I don't believe in superstition. I'm a scientist—a biology teacher."

"Science can't explain everything."

Being a ranger, alone in the national parks for many hours per week, he'd learned to prepare for the exceptions rather than trust in the rules. Mother Nature was an unpredictable old broad. Just when he thought he had things figured out, his expectations would be turned upside down. When he set out tonight, he'd never thought he'd meet a woman with the cheerful name of Daisy Brighton who was looking for a gold bullion in a graveyard. Never thought he'd be attracted to her wide, confident smile and her irritation when she tucked messy strands of her curly blond hair behind her ear. He liked that she was an organized woman and got a kick out of how annoyed she seemed when things got out of hand. She'd be fun to tease.

With his flashlight, he pointed downhill toward a tumbledown stone wall surrounding a clearing at the edge of the forest. "That's the boot hill over there."

"How do you know?"

"I've been here before. That's what park rangers do. We range. And we explore. The campground is only a mile from here through those trees." Again, he used the beam of his flashlight as a pointer. "Listen."

She went silent and appeared to concentrate. "I hear it. Do you have to go back and shut down the party?"

"Not yet. I told them they could play their music until ten thirty."

Taking care of drunk and disorderly campers wasn't his usual job as an investigator, but Carter had added an extra layer of vigilance, personally checking out every complaint. A couple of people reported a Peeping Tom, some guy in a ski mask. It was his job to protect those who came to enjoy nature—the innocent hikers, sightseers and campers. He glanced at Daisy and added treasure hunters to his list.

She swooped her flashlight in a circle. "I think I see a marker over there to the left. I'll hike down and take a closer look."

"I'll start at the opposite side," he said. "We can meet in the middle."

Ambient light from the moon and stars helped him find his way to the remnants of a low stone wall. Four ponderosa pines loomed over the graves at the northern edge. Shrubs and high grasses had taken over much of the cemetery. He found a cluster of weathered wooden crosses with the names rewritten in black lettering. These four graves were occupied by the same outlaw gang.

He called out to her, "Are you okay?"

"I'm a lot better off than this guy whose marker says he was killed by a moose."

He moved closer to the trees and heard the rippling from a creek. He crinkled his nose. The night breeze carried a rotten stench. He might be having a premonition of his own. When he peered into the forest, he saw a reflection from the watching eyes of a nocturnal predator, probably a coyote or a wolf. Why would a night hunter lurk so close to humans? He unsnapped the safety strap on his belt holster, making it easier to draw his Beretta if it became necessary.

Looking down, he saw that someone had gone to the trouble of outlining a grave site with stones. Carter took care to walk around the edges rather than stepping on a final resting place. He was probably more superstitious than Daisy.

Before walking to the middle of the boot hill, he returned to the north edge to make sure he'd seen everything. Beside a clump of chokecherries, he found an open grave. Shallow, it couldn't have been more than five inches deep. The woman who lay supine on the overturned soil had been dead long enough to attract predators. Her flesh was torn. Half her face was gone. The blood on her clothing had dried to ugly brown stains. In the moonlight, her skin took on a gray-blue tint, deeper in places from bruising. The stench of putrefied flesh clogged his nostrils. He saw a wound at her neck that was partially covered by a flowing silk scarf.

Two weeks ago, he'd seen another body laid out and similarly displayed at a graveyard in Glenwood Springs. Her name was Hannah Guerrero. She'd also worn a scarf.

"Carter, come here." Daisy's voice trembled. "Hurry. I found a woman. She's dead."

A third victim.

According to the FBI, three murders meant they were looking for a serial killer.

Chapter Two

In the boot hill, at the edge of the forest, Daisy crouched beside the body of a woman lying on the ground with her legs stretched out. Her flashlight lay beside her with the beam shining through the tall grass toward stone and wooden markers. Aware that the young woman was very likely dead and should be left untouched for the CSI investigators, Daisy was compelled to feel for a pulse. Her flesh felt cold. A delicate butterfly tattoo floated above her wrist. No pulse.

The onset of rigor mortis had tightened her muscles and caused her jaw to clench. Her eyelids squeezed shut. Her long, straight brown hair fanned out around her face. A pretty face, not peaceful in death but tense and somehow frightened.

The person who had arranged the body—the murderer—had taken care with her, making sure the buttons on her blouse were fastened and her khaki slacks weren't bunched or wrinkled. Bright red blood glistened on the wound that slashed across her throat. A long, flower-patterned silk scarf tied around her neck obscured most of the laceration. The freshness of the blood made Daisy wonder if the killer was still nearby.

She peeked over her shoulder and peered into the

deep, dark forest. Anyone could be hiding there. *Cougars, coyotes and bears, oh my.* Again, she called out, "I need you, Carter."

"I'm on my way."

She placed the woman's hand across her flat stomach, where it had been before. "I'm so sorry," Daisy whispered. She didn't believe the dead woman could hear her words but wanted to show respect. "I hope your life was well lived."

Though adrenaline pumped through her, Daisy didn't experience feelings of shock or fear. This wasn't her first dead body. When she was in high school taking an advanced placement biology class, she'd been lucky enough to share a cadaver with other students. Since then, she'd seen other corpses in college-level classes or at the body farm where she studied forensic anatomy.

She stood and picked up her flashlight. Newly killed, this victim was unique in her experience. Daisy wiped the nervous sweat from her forehead. Facing this dead woman disturbed her more than studying a medically prepared body laid out on an examination table. Surely, there was something she could learn. Slowly and deliberately, she directed the beam from the top of the woman's head to the scarf and death wound, then down her body to her feet, which were bare. Leaning down, she inspected the soles. Not dirty at all.

As Carter approached, she noticed that he walked in a zigzag pattern to avoid stepping on graves. *Superstitious?* When he came close, his flashlight beam shone on her, then the body, then back to her. "I'll be damned. Another one."

"What do you mean?"

"On the other side of the cemetery, I stumbled across a shallow grave. Another dead woman."

"A serial killer?"

"Could be." Though she couldn't see his eyes under his cowboy hat, she felt his gaze assessing her as he said, "You seem calm. Doesn't this upset you?"

"Of course it does. Murder is a terrible thing. But…"

"What?"

"I teach biology, and I usually get cadavers for my students. Those bodies are medically prepped for us to study, but they're still dead people."

"Uh-huh."

"And I've also taken classes and worked at the body farm outside Denver, where the dead are buried in different conditions and left for students to study. The smell there is—well, it's something else."

"Uh-huh."

"Anyway, I don't believe this woman was killed at this location. Look here—you can see that her bare feet are clean. She didn't walk through the forest or the grass."

He leaned down to see. In the reflected glow of the flashlight, she noticed that his skin had paled under his tan. His lips pinched tightly together in the tense expression of a person who was holding on to self-control with both hands to keep from losing it.

"Good observation," he said in a coarse voice. "You're right about the feet."

His squeamish reaction surprised her. She'd figured that—in his work as a ranger—he was either a hunter or familiar with their procedures, like field dressing and skinning an elk, which was way more gruesome than this. Also, since he worked as an investigator, he'd certainly seen dead bodies before. "Sorry, Carter. I didn't mean to gross you out."

"I'm fine." He pointed his flashlight up the hill. "Walk with me. I need to go to my car and radio headquarters for backup support."

"Doesn't your cell phone work?"

"Reception is spotty around here." He took a couple of backward steps and waited for her to do the same before hiking toward the ghost town.

For a moment, they walked without speaking. The crunching sound of their footsteps on dry pine needles mingled with other noises—the distant echo of music from the campground, the breeze whispering through the pine boughs and the incessant skittering of nocturnal creatures. And killers. Was he close? Had he been watching them?

Carter hadn't asked for her opinion but hadn't told her to pipe down. She volunteered another comment. "If I had to make an educated guess, I'd say time of death was no more than three hours ago, probably more like two."

"Why is that?"

"The blood at her throat is fresh, rigor mortis is just starting to set in and there's minimal evidence of flies, maggots or animal predators."

"I've got to tell you, Daisy, you're not what I expected." He stopped beside the broken-down chimney at the edge of Butcher's Gulch, took off his hat and raked his fingers through his thick black hair. "I thought you were a city woman visiting her auntie and poking around at Western history. After a couple of weeks, I figured you'd be bored and run back to Denver."

She had to admit that he wasn't altogether wrong.

"I'm not deeply invested in the search for Brighton's Bullion. But my aunt Vi is my last living relative, and I care about her enough to make the effort."

"There's something more to your visit than spending time with family," he said. "You were drawn to the mountains. You're not panicky about finding a body because you consider death to be natural. You aren't nervous about coyotes or bears."

She wasn't sure if he was complimenting her or making fun of her. "What are you trying to tell me, Carter?"

"I'm saying you fit in. You're comfortable here."

"Maybe or maybe not. I've always lived in the city." Every morning she awoke with the sun and happily greeted the majestic outline of the front range of the Rockies from her bedroom window, but she had no desire to come here like a pioneer and settle into a log cabin. "Did you grow up in the mountains?"

"I was a cop in Denver before I became a ranger." He replaced the hat on his head. "I love my job, and I'm usually good at it. I kind of hate that I got queasy. And that you pointed it out. You're a little bit pushy."

"Guilty." As if she needed his approval.

"I'm not judging."

"No?"

"I like you, Daisy."

His statement was simple, direct and totally charming. It took a confident man to leave himself so vulnerable. What if she shot him down? Or the opposite, she might take his comment as an invitation to sex. Confused, she said, "Thank you?"

"I appreciate your intelligence, and I'd be a damn fool if I didn't take advantage of your expertise. What else can you tell me about the dead woman?"

Relieved, she returned to a topic she knew something about. "When I first arrived, I took her hand to feel for a pulse. I noticed her fingernail polish was chipped, and one nail was torn. Makes me think that she fought for her life."

"Anything else?"

"There was a strange smell. Not the typical aromas I associate with the dead."

"I noticed it, too," he said. "Bear repellent. I don't put much stock in dousing your campsite with weird combinations of ammonia, garlic, sulfur and other stuff, but there are people who swear it will keep the animals and the insects away."

She made the logical assumption. "The killer must have used repellent because he didn't want predators to damage her body. That fits with the way he arranged her and fixed her hair."

"And tied a scarf around her throat. The other body also had a scarf. I wonder why." He frowned. "Maybe it'd be useful to consult a profiler."

A profiler? Talking with that type of expert could be extremely interesting. In spite of her respect for the dead woman, Daisy felt a glimmer of selfish excitement. She could be part of a murder investigation. *Cool!*

Headlights flashed behind Carter's SUV as Jackknife's beat-up truck pulled up and parked. The old man jumped out, spat tobacco juice, waved his scrawny arm and hollered, "Howdy, sweet thang. I'm back. Bet you're glad to see me."

Carter aimed his flashlight into the grizzled face. "Stop right there."

When the beam hit Jackknife, he squinted. "You got a problem, sonny boy?"

"NPS Ranger Carter," he identified himself. "Show me your registration and license."

"It's okay," Daisy assured him. "This is Mr. Jones. He drove me here."

"And left you without a ride. Not a real nice guy." His flashlight didn't waver. "I need your identification."

The old man spat again. "If'n I don't feel like showing it, what's gonna happen?"

With lightning speed, Carter flipped his flashlight to his left hand. With his right, he drew his Beretta. "Hands on top of your head, Jones. I don't have time to play games."

If Jackknife considered fighting back, that notion disappeared when Carter took a determined step toward him. The ranger wasn't goofing around, and Jackknife knew it. He put both hands on top of his John Deere cap with the leaping stag logo. "I'll do whatever you say, Ranger. I'll cooperate."

In a few efficient moves, Carter cuffed Jackknife with his hands in front, took his car keys and helped him climb into the driver's seat of his truck. "Stay here until I have time to take your statement."

"Statement about what? What the heck is going on here?"

"Murder investigation," Carter said.

"Somebody got killed?" His voice creaked into a higher octave. "I don't know nothing about it. Tell him, Daisy."

She opened her mouth to speak, but before she could get a word out, Jackknife continued, "And what about her, huh? If'n I can't drive, how's she gonna get home?"

"I'll arrange for her ride," Carter said.

"I couldn't ask you to do that now," she said, not wanting to be a bother in the middle of an investigation. "It's a long way back to Leadville."

"What are you talking about?" He shot her a puzzled glance. "It's only about forty minutes—less because there's no traffic or snow."

"Only forty minutes, huh?" She glared at Jackknife. "We were in your truck for more than twice that long."

"Mebbe I got lost."

More likely, he was playing a joke on her. *Not funny.* "I suggest you get comfortable in that rattletrap truck, because Ranger Carter has a lot of work to do before he talks to you."

She turned her back on him and strode toward the NPS vehicle.

Carter came up beside her. "How well do you know that guy?"

"Not well at all."

"Do you have any reason to suspect him?"

She couldn't believe her aunt would let her get into the truck with Jackknife if she thought he was up to no good. But Aunt Vi wouldn't count this grungy, tobacco-spitting old man as a friend. "He's kind of a jerk but probably harmless."

"That's how the neighbors of serial killers always describe them. They always say that the monster was harmless, a nice guy who kept to himself and wouldn't hurt a fly."

She reconsidered. If her time-of-death analysis was accurate, Jackknife could have murdered that woman and returned to Leadville before he picked her up. They were on the road for over an hour and a half before they got close to Butcher's Gulch. Why would Jackknife purposely delay? Why would he drive around in circles? A possible answer hit her—he might have been waiting for darkness to fall.

He might have planned a murder scenario for her. Shivers scampered across her back like a herd of spiders. "Jackknife Jones could be the killer."

"Jackknife, huh? I don't even want to guess how he got that nickname." Carter opened the driver's side door of his car. "I'll be with you in a minute. I need to put through a call to headquarters."

She had a similar thought. Her aunt deserved a call so she wouldn't worry, but Daisy's cell phone still didn't have reception. Earlier when they were driving to Butcher's Gulch in Carter's SUV, she'd noticed a bunch of screens and communication devices attached to the center console, including a heavy-looking phone on a charger—a satellite phone, too bulky to carry in your pocket but essential in areas without good access to cell phone towers.

Standing just outside the open driver's side door, she watched as he took that phone rather than using his police radio that would alert anyone listening on that open line. Apparently, he wanted privacy when he talked to headquarters.

"Excuse me," she said. "Can I use your sat phone to call my aunt?"

"When I'm done." Taking the phone with him, he left the car, locked the door and started back toward the boot hill. "Come with me. Stay close."

Further warning was unnecessary. She'd seen the murdered woman and knew there was a killer at large. If not Jackknife, then who? There didn't seem to be anyone living in this area. When she scanned the forested hills and rocky cliffs, she didn't see house lights. Could they have come from the campground?

She half listened while Carter rattled off instructions to NPS headquarters. He wanted assistance from the local sheriff's office, the state highway patrol and agents from the FBI. He repeated "FBI" twice and added, "Tell them we're looking for a serial killer. They need to arrange for the autopsies."

Plural—as in more than one. She shuddered and fidgeted. Though she stayed close to Carter, Daisy wandered through the graves, shining her flashlight beam on the markers. This side of the cemetery featured several fieldstone markers with names roughly chiseled and occasional embellishments, usually angels or hearts and flowers. Daisy tripped over a chunk of granite that was almost completely obscured by the high grasses. Kneeling, she lowered her flashlight beam and read the inscription: "Annie Brighton. Wife, Friend and Lover."

There was no date of birth or death. No indication of what killed her. But Daisy knew she'd found the final resting place of Sherwood Brighton's wife.

Chapter Three

Ranger A. P. Carter ended his call to Joaquin Stanley, his supervisor at the National Park Service headquarters in Salida, and hiked through the graves to where Daisy knelt beside a tombstone. She shook her flashlight at a rugged stone, causing the beam to flicker. "Read it."

"'Annie Brighton. Wife, Friend and Lover.'" He wasn't thinking about treasure hunting. Not now. The double—no, triple—murder investigation would be hell to coordinate among the several law enforcement jurisdictions and would take his full attention. "Is this good news or bad?"

"It's unexpected. I was looking for Sherwood, not his wife, and I don't know much about her. Also, this marker is sort of vindication for Jackknife. He wasn't lying about seeing the name in the Butcher's Gulch boot hill."

"Don't be so quick to forgive. There's no explanation for why he pretended to be lost."

"I'm not defending him. Jackknife is a total jerk but probably not be a serial killer." She shrugged. "May I use your sat phone to call my aunt? She'll be pleased about finding Annie."

"First, there's something I want your opinion on."

He hooked the sat phone onto his belt. "The county sheriff has been alerted, and his deputies will arrive soon. When they do, I won't be able to talk with you."

"Why? Am I going to disappear?"

"You're a civilian, Daisy. Some of these guys will try to shove you out of the way. They won't understand or accept your expertise, but I do." Holding her slender hand, he led her down the hill, hoping he wasn't making a mistake by recruiting a high school biology teacher as a consultant. "I want you to take a look at this shallow grave."

"Where is she?"

"Down this slope."

He'd debated with himself before trusting her. Though he appreciated her straightforward analysis of the other victim, he couldn't get around the fact that she wasn't a cop or a ranger or a medical examiner. He had hesitated because sharing the details of a murder smacked of unprofessional behavior. But what the hell should he do? This case was different. He'd never investigated a serial murder and had never faced the possibility of more victims being attacked if he didn't solve it quickly. Carter needed all the help he could get.

Walking slowly behind him, she pinched her nose. "This one has been dead long enough for the flesh to putrefy."

"How long is that?"

"At least three days."

Knowing the medical details before the deputies showed up gave Carter an edge. While they were gagging and puking in the forest, he could plan the strategy for his investigation. The timing of the murders—especially when combined with what he'd seen of Hannah Guerrero in Glenwood Springs—was an important factor. He rubbed at his nose, trying to erase the stench. "You know, Daisy, if you don't want to go any farther, it's okay."

"I don't mind the smell. When I was working at the body farm, I got used to it." She kept moving forward. "I'd like to ask a favor from you."

"Go ahead."

"I've never seen an actual autopsy. Can you arrange for me to watch?"

For the life of him, he couldn't figure out why he was attracted to this woman. "I can arrange for you to sit in."

Her thank-you and enthusiastic smile would have been appropriate for someone who'd been given freebie tickets on the fifty-yard line for a Denver Broncos playoff game. "Where will it take place?"

"That's up to the FBI," he said. "I'm guessing Pueblo."

At the edge of the shallow grave, he forced himself to, once again, look down at the dead woman whose clothing was ripped and bloodstained. What was left of her face appeared to be bloated, and her discolored flesh had turned a dead gray color.

Daisy crouched and slid the beam of her flashlight up and down the body. "It's hard to believe this is the handiwork of the same killer. The other woman was handled delicately, while this one looks like she was abused. The only item of clothing that appears to be clean is the long scarf around her neck. Do you see the bruises on her arms and ligature marks on her wrists? She might have been tied down. If you call in a profiler, they could draw a lot of inferences from this."

"I'll make sure we have photos of both bodies." He hadn't been so diligent with the Glenwood corpse. Not his jurisdiction. Not his case. But Daisy was correct. A profiler would add a different perspective, especially when studying similarities among the victims. They were all young and fit, average height and weight. Their coloring was different. Hannah Guerrero had black hair and olive skin. The woman Daisy found had long brown hair. This one was platinum blonde. The killer didn't seem to have a preferred type. "What else?"

Using a stick she found on the ground, Daisy lifted the hand and showed him the limp wrist. "She's already gone through rigor, and the stiffness has worn off. Like I said, time of death was probably over two or three days ago."

"Can you narrow it down?"

"Not with precision," she said. "Body temp won't be a good indicator because she's been outdoors, and temperature at this time of year fluctuates by several degrees from day to night. And I don't have a liver thermometer."

He wished real-life forensics could be as clear and infallible as portrayed on television. Hannah had been killed in Glenwood ten days ago. If this woman had been dead for three days, that meant a seven-day difference before he killed a second time. The body that Daisy found was recently murdered, which meant the interim had grown shorter.

Without hesitation, Daisy leaned close and aimed the flashlight beam at the dead woman's horribly mangled face. "Maggots. Do you see the eggs?"

Carter looked into the wound. Small, pale eggs mingled with crawly insects. "I see them." He gagged. This was as close as he'd come to vomiting at a murder scene. He would have preferred being stoic, but his nausea occurred as an automatic reflex.

"There isn't too much damage by predators. Torn clothes. Teeth and claw marks here and there. I suspect there was something shielding her body." She sat back on her heels and looked up at him. "Or she might have been murdered somewhere else. He might have allowed the blood to drain before bringing her to this shallow grave."

"Can you tell how much she bled onto the dirt below her?"

"Not without moving the body," she said, "and I don't think your medical examiner would appreciate that much interference. Also, I can't turn her to check on lividity—the way the blood settled after death."

So many questions, and he needed to find answers to all of them. If there had been something covering her and shielding her from local predators, he needed to search. If she'd been held somewhere else, he might find that the killer lived in the area. Or he could have loaded the dead woman in his car and brought her here.

He started a mental checklist: Check for tire tracks. Search for something that covered the body. Look for a shovel or spade. Search the forest in this area. So much to do and so little time before he handed over jurisdiction of the investigation.

AFTER DAISY MADE her phone call to Aunt Vi and returned the sat phone to Carter, she heard the wail of a police siren bouncing off the canyon walls. Together, she and Carter hiked up the gently sloping hill to the ghost town and greeted the deputies who emerged from an SUV with the county sheriff's logo on the door. Though she stood ready and willing to help, the two officers—Graham and Escobar—barely acknowledged her presence. Carter had predicted that she'd be ignored as a mere civilian, and he'd been correct.

Not being a person who demanded a lot of attention, she was glad to step back and quietly observe what was happening. Deputy Graham—a clean-shaven, athletic-looking man in a dark green uniform and a baseball cap with the county logo—brightened when Carter told them they might be dealing with a serial killer. He immediately covered his unacceptable grin with a scowl, but she'd seen his excitement, and she understood. Serial killers were strange and terrifying creatures. Legendary, like boogiemen or vampires, they haunted nightmares and struck fear in the hearts of average citizens. Tracking one down meant a major challenge for a young deputy in a mainly rural county.

Carter asked, "Do you have lights for the crime scene?"

"Sure do," Graham replied as he hooked his thumbs in his belt on either side of a shiny rodeo championship buckle for bronc riding.

"How about some of those throwaway booties so we don't mess up footprints?"

"I got those and latex gloves, too."

"Let's gather the gear and set up at the location of the first body."

"There's more than one." Graham stated the obvious description of a serial killer. "Are they all in the graveyard?"

"Two are here. Ten days ago, there was a third." Carter turned to the other deputy, a middle-aged guy wearing the uniform shirt with weathered jeans and boots. "I'd appreciate if you stay here and meet the others who have been contacted."

Cool and casual, Deputy Escobar nodded. "We'll have another vehicle from our office. And I expect you contacted the NPS, so there will be a couple of rangers. Who else?"

"State patrol, coroner, ambulance and FBI. Could be more than that. My supervisor made the calls." Carter matched the calm, controlled attitude of the older lawman. "I don't want a herd of investigators trooping through the graveyard messing up evidence. If you need more information about what we're dealing with, you can talk with Ms. Brighton."

She straightened her shoulders, glad to be helpful, and gave a small wave to the deputy. Escobar signaled for her to come closer. "Want some coffee, Brighton?"

"Call me Daisy. And yes on the coffee."

He led her to the passenger side of the SUV, pulled out a long silver thermos and poured hot liquid into a disposable cup. "I hope you like it black. My wife sends me out the door with plenty of sandwiches and strong coffee when I'm on night shift."

"Black is perfect." She sipped. Even though the coffee wasn't delicious, she knew the caffeine would lift her spirits. "Thanks, Deputy. Do you have any questions?"

He leaned against the front bumper of his vehicle and watched as Carter and the younger deputy gathered equipment from the back. "What were you doing in the graveyard?"

"Research," she said as though it was the most normal thing in the world to be poking around in a graveyard after dark. "Carter was kind enough to help me, and I found the first body."

"That must have scared you."

"Not at all."

She rattled through an explanation about being a biology teacher who regularly handled cadavers and segued into forensic descriptions of the two murdered women. Occasionally, Escobar asked questions, and she answered as best she could.

She had a question of her own. "Have you worked with Carter before?"

"A couple of times. He's a good man." He tasted his coffee and slanted a wise glance in her direction. "You like him."

"I didn't say that."

"Didn't need to. Your eyes did the talking." He grinned. "And why not? You two go together like peanut butter and jelly. You're both smart and good-looking. You're both concerned about other folks."

"How do you figure?"

"He's a ranger. You're a teacher. Caretakers."

"There's nothing going on between me and Carter."

She truly wished relationships could be as simple as matching a few personality traits, but she'd never found attraction to be easy, and she hadn't really had enough time to analyze the possibilities. Of course, she found Carter to be physically appealing. He was tall and lean and looked like the romantic archetype of a cowboy in his hat, boots and jeans. The curly black hair, expressive eyes and great smile were additional pluses. If she'd been younger, she might have jumped into a brief fling with the ranger, but she was twenty-nine and ready for something more than a quickie—as Aunt Vi would say, "a roll in the hay." Daisy wanted to settle down, get serious and start a family.

Nothing long-term would work between her and

Carter. He was a mountain man. And she was a city woman.

She was saved from further embarrassing conversation with Escobar by the arrival of three vehicles: one from the park service, another from the county sheriff and a patrol car with the Colorado state logo on the door and red and blue flashers whirring on the roof. The officers, rangers and deputies gathered around while Escobar told them to stay put until Carter came back up the hill and explained the situation. "He doesn't want y'all tromping around and messing up the evidence." Escobar craned his neck, scanning the group. "I don't suppose there's a coroner here."

"We heard this was a serial killer," one of the state police officers said.

The two rangers complained that this was really their crime scene, and they needed to be with Carter. There was more grumbling all around.

"Settle down," Escobar said. "Ms. Brighton, would you mind heading down to the site and telling Carter to come up here?"

She was delighted to walk away from the impatient crew of rangers and officers. Though she'd already made a couple of trips through the graveyard, she still needed her flashlight until she got close to where Carter and Graham had positioned two portable, battery-operated units that spotlighted the scene like a movie set. Though she saw more details, the body looked as unreal as the plastic cadavers she sometimes used for her classes.

Graham stood as far away from the dead woman as possible without disappearing into the shadows while Carter got in close and personal to inspect the fatal wound at her throat. His queasiness seemed to have diminished. He waved her over. "Daisy, take a look at this."

When she leaned down beside him, she caught a whiff of the mentholated gel that was supposed to mask the stink of bear repellent and death. Graham must have brought it. "What did you want to show me?"

With latex gloves covering both hands, he gently separated the scarf from the blood. "There are already insect eggs."

"Blowflies," she said. "They're drawn by the smell of carrion and show up immediately."

He ordered the deputy to make sure he took close-up photos. To her, he said, "There's a crowd gathering at the top of the hill."

"That's why I'm interrupting you. Escobar could use some help dealing with them."

"Has the FBI arrived?"

"Not yet," she said. "Why do you ask?"

"With their state-of-the-art databases and forensic equipment, they typically assume jurisdiction on serial murders. I need to talk to the feds before I hand over control."

"It doesn't seem fair for you to just step aside."

"What's fair is finding the killer before he strikes again," he said as he stood. "You're not wearing your booties."

"My bad." She rose tilted her head to gaze into his vivid blue eyes. This was the first time she'd gotten a good look at him in clear light, and she wasn't disappointed. The spotlights for the crime scene reflected off his high cheekbones and the smile that hid his true nature as a sharp, decisive man. Was that also a trait they shared? She suspected it was. She and Carter were both people who got things done.

Whoops and laughter resonated from the thick pine forest beyond boot hill. She saw Pinkie step away from the trees followed by several others from the party at the campground. They were about a hundred yards away.

Carter whirled and started toward them. "Daisy, come with me. Graham, go up to the top of the hill and tell the crew that one person from each vehicle can come down here."

"They need to wear gloves and booties," Graham said.

"Make sure they do. That's your responsibility."

Daisy followed as he marched toward the raucous partygoers, who must have followed the path from the campground. The woman with pink hair appeared to be their leader. She gave an enthusiastic but sloppy-drunk wave. "Hey there, Mr. Ranger. What's with all the cop cars?"

"There's an investigation underway." Carter continued to stride toward them. Even in his baby blue paper booties, he exuded authority.

"Cool!" Pinkie said. "What kind of investigation?"

As they approached the group of five people, Daisy recognized some of them from the party—three men, Pinkie and one other woman with red hair in two ponytails. One of the guys seemed totally wasted, but the other two were alert. The tallest, a husky guy with a buzz cut, looked a bit older than the others, maybe in his early thirties. He explained, "We heard the sirens and wanted to find out what was going on."

"That's her." Pinkie jabbed her index finger in Daisy's direction. "She's the lady who's a treasure hunter."

"Brighton's Bullion," said the tall guy. "Had any luck?"

"Not really." No point in telling him about Sherwood's wife's grave.

The other relatively sober guy squinted through horn-rimmed glasses and tried to step around Carter. "There's lights set up over there. It looks like a body on the ground."

With his arms spread wide, Carter herded them back toward the trail. "I need you to stay out of the way."

"Is he right?" Pinkie asked. "Was somebody murdered?"

"Yes." Carter dropped his arms. "And you're witnesses. I need information from—"

"Wait a minute." Her eyelids twitched, and she looked like she was going to cry. "Is she about my height? Does she have brown hair?"

"Yes."

"And a tattoo?" Pinkie said. "A butterfly tattoo on her left wrist."

Daisy couldn't help nodding when Pinkie looked toward her.

"Oh my God." Pinkie sobbed. "It's Rene."

Chapter Four

Carter hated the disorganized way this investigation was unfolding. Even if he didn't have the jurisdiction to hunt a serial killer, he'd hoped to hand over a coherent package of evidence to the FBI agents instead of a jumbled mess. From literally stumbling over the bodies to having a half-drunk, pink-haired woman blurt out the identity of the victim, every bit of information had come in random, unexpected bursts. Nothing—with the exception of Daisy's forensic observations—had been the result of logic or intelligent discovery. He needed to step up and take charge, even if he ultimately handed off the investigation to the FBI.

Leaving Daisy to keep an eye on the five partygoers who had stumbled out of the forest, he went to the boot hill to wrangle the crew of law enforcement personnel. His assignment for the state patrolman was to take fingerprints from the victim and run her photo through facial recognition software to get a solid identification. The deputies were given forensic tasks, and he sent the rangers back to the campground to take statements before the partygoers dispersed. Daisy would stay with him to record his interviews with Pinkie and her friends. *Unprofessional? Yeah, probably.* He shouldn't use a civilian for investigative business, but he needed to talk to these people before they had time to put their heads together and make sure their stories matched. One of them might slip up and say something useful. One of them could be the killer.

Their spokeswoman was Pinkie. The death of her friend had sobered her up, and she gave cogent answers to his questions. The woman with the butterfly tattoo was Rene Williams, twenty-three years old and a part-time student at the University of Colorado campus in Denver, as were most of the attendees at the party. Rene had gone missing the night before last, but nobody worried about her absence. She'd come on this camping trip to escape her depression after breaking up with her boyfriend. "I thought she wanted to be alone," Pinkie said. "That was why she left."

"Do you have a phone number and address for the boyfriend?" Carter asked.

"I don't. He and Rene lived together, but he moved out a week ago. I never knew his phone number. Do you think he…" She sucked down a breath of mountain air and forced herself to continue. "Did he kill her?"

"Too early to speculate. How long have you been camping?"

"The original group, including Rene, has been here for four days. We're all going back to Denver tomorrow."

The conditions for these interviews couldn't have been much worse. All five of these people were functioning at varying levels of intoxication. They could overhear each other. And he only had a small recorder and spiral notebook to keep track of what they said. *Definitely not ideal.*

He considered backing off, waiting for the FBI agents

to swoop in and take over. The evidence he uncovered would be checked and rechecked anyway. He felt a light squeeze on his arm and gazed down at Daisy. The spark of intelligence in her light green eyes encouraged him more than a pep talk. She didn't need to say out loud that she believed in him. Her attitude radiated confidence. He suspected that she was a hell of a good teacher.

"The guy with the buzz cut," she said, "might be one of the last people to see Rene alive. His name is Slade Franklin."

He grinned, glad that he had this smart, lovely civilian for backup. "You're paying attention."

"I remember what you said about finding the killer before he attacked anyone else. It's up to you, Carter, to protect the people in this forest."

A big job, and he might not be up to the challenge. But she was right. He had to try. Turning toward the others, he waved the big guy over. "Slade Franklin, join us."

After Daisy read back her notes and repeated his name and address in Pueblo, Slade took a seat on a sawed-off tree stump that stood taller than the sagebrush. Carter remained standing for this interrogation. "Tell me about the last time you saw Rene."

"She wasn't hanging around with the others. She looked lonely, and I felt bad for her. So I went over and talked to her."

"You didn't know her before you came to the party."

"No, sir."

"What did you talk about?"

"Her dumbass ex-boyfriend. I never met the guy, but I can tell you right now that he didn't deserve Rene. There was something about her that made me think I'd met her before."

"But you hadn't."

"No."

Carter asked, "Did you think she might go out with you?"

"I guess so. She didn't have any problem going skinny-dipping."

"Both naked?"

"Naw, she wore her underpants and bra. We went to my camper truck to change afterward. She was real pretty." He gave a sheepish grin. "I knew it was a bad idea to date a woman who was getting over a breakup, but I didn't care."

"Did you try to kiss her?" Carter considered the possibility of Slade making an unwanted advance on Rene. "Maybe you rubbed her back while she was changing clothes."

"She didn't want me to get close, and I had to back off. My mama taught me to be polite." In spite of his size and his buzz cut, Slade seemed to be a sensitive guy. "I know what it feels like to get dumped. It's miserable."

"Then what happened with Rene?"

"We left the campground and went to a nearby lake. It's called Teacup on account of its small and almost perfectly round. She gave me some good advice about my relationship with my ex. And then her boyfriend showed up."

Carter checked his notes. "Josh Santana?"

"Yeah, it was Josh. He grabbed her and started kissing her, and she seemed to like it, even though she told me he was a jerk."

"That must have made you mad."

"It sure did."

Carter's sat phone buzzed. Caller ID showed a name he didn't recognize. "Excuse me, I need to get this."

The call came from the Pueblo-based FBI agents assigned to the investigation. They were on the road but lost, which wasn't a big surprise. The locals could easily find the ghost town, but Butcher's Gulch wasn't on regular maps. He told the agents to track the campground on their GPS, and the rangers who were there could give them directions.

When he returned, he found Daisy asking questions. "Are you a student, Slade?"

"No, ma'am. I'm thirty-one, and I work as a carpenter."

"How did you hear about the party?"

"I didn't," he said. "I came up here in my truck camper to get away from the heat in Pueblo. It's only June, but it's hotter than August. The mountains are always ten degrees cooler."

"By yourself?" she asked with just enough edge to suggest there might be something strange about a solo trip.

"Nothing wrong with that." Taken aback, he scowled at her. "You came here alone, didn't you? Somebody might think it was strange for you to be hanging around in a graveyard."

"I couldn't leave."

"Why not?"

"Because, Mr. Franklin, I found the body."

Until she allowed him to turn the focus back on her, she'd been doing a good job, even though she wasn't a trained investigator. Carter stepped in to derail this line of questioning. "Sorry for the interruption."

"No problem."

"Let's go back to what happened at the lake, Slade." Carter used the other man's first name to emphasize that the ranger was the person in authority. "After Josh arrived, did you go back to the campsite?"

"I didn't feel like socializing. I went to my camper and hit the sack." He exhaled a heavy sigh. "Maybe I sat outside for a while and watched for Rene. But I never saw her, never again."

Flashing lights and a siren from the direction of the many vehicles in the ghost town announced the arrival of an ambulance. Though these victims had no need for paramedics, the ambulance might be needed to transport the bodies to a place designated by the FBI for autopsies. They still had to wait for the coroner and/or medical examiner.

Carter kept juggling as fast as he could, but his interviews with the other three people were rushed. Over objections from Pinkie and Slade who wanted to stay close to the action, he sent them back to the campground and told them to report to the rangers on-site.

He motioned to Daisy. Together, they returned to Butcher's Gulch, where the paramedics stood beside Deputy Escobar's vehicle. They were staring at him, challenging him with their gazes. Again, he felt the pressure of being in charge, figuring out who should do what.

Daisy said, "I'd like to help."

She didn't belong here. A high school biology teacher and part-time treasure hunter had no business taking part in a murder investigation, but he wanted her to stay, wanted to hear her opinion after the dust settled. He seized on the only excuse he could think of. "You can't leave until the FBI takes your statement. After that, I'll arrange for a ride to Leadville."

"I'd rather wait until you can take me."

He was exceedingly glad to hear it. "It could be late."

"Don't care." She shrugged. "I have a vested interest, after all. You promised I could watch an autopsy."

"Fine with me." More than fine, actually. Though practically a stranger, she seemed like the only friendly face in this crowd. He handed her his car keys. "If you want to get away from the chaos, feel free to hide out in my car."

When another SUV joined the others, the ghost town began to resemble a backwoods parking lot. Unlike the other vehicles, this black Chevy Tahoe had no special logo. It dodged around the ambulance, the state police car, the deputy's SUV, the two from the National Park Service and Jackknife's beat-up truck. When they parked, two men emerged. Both wore black vests with *FBI* stenciled on the back. Without waiting to consult with anybody else, they stormed down the hill toward the body. The feds were here to take control and catch the killer.

DAISY AVOIDED THE FBI and the paramedics, making a beeline for Deputy Escobar, who still leaned against the fender of his SUV. Apparently, his task was to direct all these people to the various sites, and he didn't seem to mind playing the role of traffic cop. She guessed his age was close to fifty, old enough to have developed a thick skin and a steady calm.

From the corner of her eye, she watched Carter shake hands with the special agents. One of them seemed to know him, but they weren't friendly. In the hierarchy of local law enforcement, the feds had to be the top of the food chain. Carter had readily admitted that they had the best experts and equipment.

Standing beside Escobar, she had a sweeping view of the boot hill and noticed that the second body site was also illuminated by the portable spotlights. She glanced at the man beside her. "I bet you've seen this before."

"Whenever there's a major crime, everybody comes sniffing around. Hail, hail, the gang's all here."

"Have you ever investigated a serial killer before?"

"Never have." He folded his arms across his chest. "And I've never heard of a killer who left his victims in a graveyard. You know there was another one, didn't you?"

She nodded. "Two women."

"Three bodies," he said. "There was another in Glenwood Springs. Three of them. That's why the murderer counts as a serial killer."

"I think Carter might have mentioned it. But he didn't give me details."

"Do you want to hear?"

She bobbed her head. "But first, I remember that you mentioned sandwiches."

"There's a cooler in the back seat. Help yourself."

Escobar was, by far, her favorite among all the investigators…except for Carter, of course. She stuck her head into the back, found the heavy-duty thermal cooler, unzipped the top and peeked inside. Escobar's wife had packed six meat-and-cheese sandwiches with sliced tomatoes and lettuce in plastic bags to the side.

She called out to him. "Do you want anything?"

"I'm sticking to coffee. Help yourself to bottled water."

As she added the tomatoes and lettuce to her basic

sandwich, Daisy realized that she hadn't eaten since lunch. She hadn't planned to spend so much time being lost with Jackknife, finding bodies and recording information from suspects. Nor had she expected to run into someone like Ranger A. P. Carter, who made her want to stay even later and spend time with him.

She returned to stand beside Escobar. "Thanks so much. I'm hungry."

"Even after looking at dead bodies?"

"Yup."

"You're a strange one," he said. "I wish my kids had a teacher like you. Somebody who makes learning fun."

"I love my job." She chomped into the sandwich. Hadn't Carter said something exactly like that about liking what he did for a living? They had so much in common. Too bad he lived in the mountains and she in town. Daisy wasn't a fan of long-distance relationships.

"The first victim," Escobar said, "was found about ten days ago in the Linwood Cemetery in Glenwood Springs. I saw it in police reports. She was lying in the dirt outside the wrought iron fence around the marker for Doc Holliday."

"Have you been to the grave?"

"Took the kids. My wife said it was educational. The legend on the marker says, 'Died in Bed.' A disappointment to Doc, because he wanted to die in action."

The ongoing commotion in the Butcher's Gulch boot hill and the many different law enforcement entities made her wonder about jurisdiction in that first murder. "Why was Carter involved? I thought crimes committed in cemeteries were investigated by the city."

"Glenwood Springs PD," he said with a nod. "The Park Service was called to consult because of the unusual layout of Linwood Cemetery. To reach the memorial for Doc Holliday, you have to hike almost a mile through a forest."

"Like Buffalo Bill Cody," she said. "Do you know about him? He's buried on top of Lookout Mountain outside Denver."

"Doc Holliday wasn't much like Cody. Buffalo Bill was a showman. Doc was a gunslinger, famous for the part he played in the shootout at the OK Corral and flat broke when he died. His part of the cemetery was a potter's field for poor folks."

"Sad." She sighed. "Doc Holliday didn't get really famous until the movies."

Escobar chuckled under his breath. "Remember that line from *Tombstone*? About being someone's huckleberry. In the movie, Doc says that to Wyatt."

Meaning Doc would follow his friend anywhere like Tom Sawyer and Huckleberry Finn. She wondered if that sentiment might apply to her and Carter. Hopefully not. She wanted to be more than a pal. She wanted to press herself into his embrace and feel his lips against hers. Pushing those thoughts aside, she said, "We've gotten off topic."

"Not much else to say about the victim in Glenwood. Her name was Hannah Guerrero, and she was a dental assistant."

"Wasn't Doc Holliday a dentist?"

"Irony."

She noticed that yet another vehicle had parked at the end of the line of cars winding through Butcher's Gulch. An older man carrying an old-fashioned doctor's bag ambled toward them. Escobar introduced her to the county coroner, a retired general practitioner with a thick white mustache. The coroner nodded to the deputy and asked what was going on.

Graciously, the deputy deferred to her. "Ms. Brighton discovered the first body. She's a biology teacher and can give you details on the medical stuff."

"I can sum it up in one word—dead." She appreciated the gesture from Escobar but didn't want to mislead this former doctor. "Is there anything specific you want to know?"

"I doubt I'll have enough accurate information for the death certificate. The ME will have to fill in the blanks." He shrugged. "Can you tell me how these women died?"

"Homicide," she said. "There were bloody wounds at the throat, but I can't say for sure that cause of death was exsanguination."

His bushy eyebrows lifted, and she saw respect dawning. "What about time of death?"

She ran through her observations on body temp, onset of rigor, bloating, skin discoloration and the presence of blowfly eggs and maggots. "But I agree with you. The actual TOD is better left to the medical examiner."

One of the paramedics joined their group. "You need to sign off on the bodies so we can figure out whether or not we need to transport them."

"Well, that's going to depend on who's in charge— the county sheriff's deputies, the Colorado state patrol, FBI or NPS."

With the investigation spinning in so many different directions, she couldn't imagine how Carter was going to proceed. After she thanked Escobar for the sandwich, Daisy made her way through the array of vehicles to Carter's SUV. Jackknife's truck was parked directly behind him, and the old man yelled at her as she came close. She blocked out his words. He was not her problem.

Glad that Carter had the foresight to give her access to his car, she opened the door using his key fob, slipped into the rear and stretched out across three seats. Though the night wasn't cold, she was glad to find a plaid wool blanket and a pillow. If Carter had attempted to sleep back here, he would have been totally uncomfortable. Though she was slightly taller than average, she fit nicely.

Before she fell asleep, her imagination conjured up an image of herself lying beside Carter with his arms encircling her. She was ready for sweet dreams.

Chapter Five

Daisy jolted awake when the car parked. The engine continued to hum, and she heard triumphant instrumental music from the CD player. *A soundtrack? For what?* Her eyelids blinked open, and she remembered climbing into the back seat of Carter's SUV. Sitting up, she held the plaid wool blanket in front of her to block the chill. Outside the windows, she saw a wall of trees.

She shook off the vestiges of sleep, stretched her spine and rotated her shoulders. Daisy had always been a morning person, quickly alert. "Where are we?"

"Not too far from Butcher's Gulch," Carter said as he twisted around in his seat to look at her. "It's after five thirty, the edge of dawn."

"So early."

"Or late," he said, "depending on your point of view."

Last night when she curled up in here, it had been before midnight. She'd slept for over five hours—must have been more tired than she realized. She inhaled a deep breath and listened to the classical music as Carter hummed along to the music from *Star Wars* by John Williams. "May the force be with you."

"I like to think it is."

Up till now, he'd kept the geekier side of his personality hidden, like his smile. But Carter was almost as nerdy as any of her high school students. "Do you think of yourself as Obi-Wan? Or Luke Skywalker?"

"Neither."

"Of course not." She groaned. "Han Solo."

"You've got to love him." He turned off the music and opened his door. "Come with me."

She didn't have time to ask where they were going. Before she had her feet planted on the ground, he was already halfway down a gradual slope. The early-morning breeze brushed against her cheeks—fresh, bracing and pine scented. With the sunrise blushing a delicate pink in the sky, flashlights weren't necessary, but she picked her way carefully until she emerged from the forest.

Standing on the rocky shore of a small lake, she watched the pastel dawn reflect on the sparkling waters and shimmer in the spiky treetops. Without saying a word, Carter stood close beside her and took her hand. Though they'd only met last night and nothing had happened between them, they shared an intimacy.

"Teacup Lake." He pointed across the crystalline waters to the north. "That's where Josh found Rene and Slade."

Her hand felt safe and warm in his unexpectedly familiar grasp. "Did you have a chance to talk to the witnesses again?"

"I did a quick interview of your buddy, Jackknife Jones. He admitted that he purposely got lost when he was driving. Somebody paid him to not take you to Butcher's Gulch until after dark."

"That's ominous. Did he say who?"

"Didn't know the guy, and I'm not sure he was telling the truth. Jackknife might have wanted to get you alone after dark."

She shuddered. "What about the others?"

"According to the one you call Pinkie, Rene used to bathe in the lake."

"Naked?"

"That's usually the way you take a bath," he said. "I talked to others at the campsite. One of the guys claimed he knew you. His name is Eric Wolff."

Irritation shot through her, and she tensed, inadvertently squeezing Carter's hand. "The Wolff family—Eric and his father, Gerald—are direct descendants of Morris Wolff, who was part of Sherwood Brighton's outlaw gang. Eric has exaggerated the role of his ancestor to partner and claims to have information that will lead to the bullion, which he thinks is half his."

"None of the others at the party recognized him as part of their regular gang."

"Like Slade Franklin," she pointed out.

"And there were a couple of other young men who were drawn to the music, free beer and women in cutoff jeans." He paused to look down at her. The first rays of the sun glowed on his cheekbones and sculpted chin. "Do you think Eric was looking for you?"

"Yes." Her gaze lowered to his lips, and she imagined what their kiss would be like—their first kiss. She looked away from him before she did something she might regret. "It can't be a coincidence that he was there."

"What else do you know about this guy?" Carter asked.

"Like my aunt, he believes the key to finding the treasure is locating Sherwood Brighton's grave." She blamed Eric and his father for her quest to locate grave sites. "His reasoning comes from letters written to Morris Wolff. I think there were a couple from Annie Brighton, Sherwood's wife. Anyway, Aunt Vi believes he's onto something."

"Did he ever mention Glenwood or Doc Holliday?"

"I don't think so." She frowned. "You're thinking of the first victim."

"Hannah Guerrero," he said.

"Was she posed in the same position as Rene and the other woman?"

"There were similarities." He turned his head to stare across the rippling waves. "Flat on her back, fully dressed with hands folded on her stomach. A long silk scarf was tied around her throat. Apparently, she'd been killed where she lay. Her blood spread across the dirt and got in her long black hair."

"Black hair?"

"She didn't resemble either of the other victims," he said. "The killer doesn't have a type."

"Was Hannah from Glenwood?"

"It was a nearby town, like Carbondale or Basalt. Her friends described her as sociable, easygoing and gullible—the kind of person who believed every crazy story, which makes me think she would have loved your treasure hunt. I wish I could have done more to find her killer."

"What did the police ask you to do?"

"To see if I could learn anything from the trail that led up to the memorial. A well-traveled path with too many footprints. Long story short—I didn't find much. No signs of a struggle. There was an imprint in the dirt of Hannah's shoes and a pair of size-thirteen sneakers."

"A big man?"

"Not necessarily," he said. "The important thing is that each of his footprints were outside hers and facing the same direction."

"How does that work?"

When she tried to move into the position the footprints indicated, he spun her around until she stood in front of him with her shoulders against his chest. "Like this," he said.

"Why?"

In answer, he slung an arm around her middle to hold her in place. With the opposite hand, he drew an imaginary blade across her throat. His action took only a few seconds. "That's one way it could have happened."

"He would have gotten blood all over his clothes."

"Unless he released her immediately." Suiting the action to the word, he dropped his arms and stepped back. "He severed the carotid. She might have staggered a few paces before she lost consciousness and fell to the ground. The blood spatters indicate that sort of scenario."

"Gruesome." Talking about the murder disturbed her a lot more than analyzing the bodily remains. She'd also been thrown off balance by their sudden physical contact. Even when he was illustrating a murder scene, Carter's nearness felt good to her.

He continued, "I also found that the killer wiped his shoes on the pine needles before he hiked down. It looked like he and Hannah walked up there together."

"Which meant he was someone she trusted."

"Or wasn't afraid to be alone with after dark."

The gap between trusting someone and not being afraid of them spread as wide as a chasm. In all the years she'd been dating, Daisy was notoriously slow to trust. Only once had she allowed a relationship to develop into living together, an arrangement that lasted only eight months. On the other hand, she was seldom afraid of being alone with a person she'd just met. Hadn't she hopped into Jackknife's truck without giving him a second thought?

She asked, "Is it possible that the killer was her boyfriend?"

"I don't remember all the details. It wasn't my case," he said. "All I've got are the basics. On the night of her murder, Hannah and her friends were at a tavern in Glenwood. She left at ten o'clock to meet a guy who was an Old West fanatic and curious about Doc Holliday's ghost."

"Sounds like Eric Wolff," she said. "I'm also pretty sure that he was the person who paid Jackknife to make sure I got to the boot hill after dark."

"One of her friends said Hannah had the feeling that she was being stalked."

"Again," Daisy said, "that's something Eric would do."

"This friend got worried when she couldn't reach Hannah on her cell phone. She went searching and found the body."

Daisy wondered if Carter would interview this friend. If he was in charge of the investigation, he'd surely start there, contacting the Glenwood PD. "Who will you be working with on that investigation?"

"The FBI has jurisdiction on serial killers." He continued to gaze across the waters as the forest came to life with the twittering of sparrows and buntings. A speckled owl swooped across the lake, ending his nocturnal hunt and disappearing into the forest. "The feds can use their cyberexperts to search for similar murders in different states and locations. And they'll do background checks on all the suspects."

"Including Jackknife?"

"He's a suspect. I'm not taking him off my list, but he isn't in the number one slot. These murders were probably the work of a younger, stronger man."

"Why do you think so?" she asked.

"I'm guessing he was boyfriend material, good-looking enough to entice Hannah into leaving her friends at the bar. And Rene Williams, the barefoot woman you found, was probably killed elsewhere and carried to her final resting place in the boot hill. She was a small woman, but it still takes muscles to carry a dead weight."

"You're good at this." She met his steady gaze. "Are you okay with not being in charge?"

"I don't miss tangling with all those different branches of law enforcement. If I'm not the boss, I have more freedom and fewer rules." He glided the back of his hand down her cheek and tilted her chin up toward him. "And I don't have to worry about confiding in a smart, pretty civilian like you."

He thinks I'm pretty. "I wouldn't want you to get in trouble."

"You're no trouble at all."

He dipped his head and kissed her lightly. The gentle pressure started a ripple of sensation that grew more intense when she arched her back and fitted her body against him. Her lungs squeezed, and she could barely catch her breath.

As their kiss continued and deepened, she melted.

Her legs turned to jelly. For a moment, she thought she'd swoon like a naive ingenue in a melodrama, but Daisy wasn't a weak-kneed damsel. Strength counted as one of her best assets. Determinedly, she stepped away from his embrace and stared at him, wide-eyed and aroused with her heart wildly palpitating. *Say something.* Her lower lip trembled. "The autopsy," she blurted. "Can I still watch the autopsy?"

"I'll do my best to arrange it."

"When?"

"Probably later today. In the afternoon."

She clung to the solid thought of seeing the autopsy as though it was a life raft in a sea of confusion. He'd have to take her to the medical examiner, which meant they'd be together, and she'd have another chance to be calm, cool and collected. "What do we do next?"

"I take you home to your aunt Vi."

She caught her breath as she climbed the hill behind him. *Inhale...exhale...inhale.* Her aunt was going to adore Carter. Since Daisy's retired parents had moved to Australia, Vi had donned the mantle of parenthood and never missed a chance to nag about how Daisy should settle down and get married. Vi would see the handsome ranger as an excellent candidate for Mr. Right.

WHILE THEY DROVE, Carter filled her in on the direction of the investigation. "This afternoon, we need to hook up with the FBI in Pueblo so you can give your statement. I've worked with one of the agents before. His name is Pat Wiley, and he's a straight shooter."

"There were two of them last night."

"The other is Mickey Hicks."

"Sounds like a cartoon character."

"That's a fairly accurate description, but he's not a mouse. He looks like Popeye."

Carter felt his eyelids drooping. He hadn't slept much last night and needed a burst of caffeine to jump-start his brain. He wasn't thinking right, which might explain why he'd kissed Daisy. Not a rational decision—he'd acted on impulse without considering the consequences. A mistake? Or the smartest move he'd ever made?

He pulled off and parked at a diner he knew had decent coffee. The food wasn't great, but he needed calories for energy. Daisy, an early bird, chowed down and chatted while downing her own coffee. Watching her gave him more vigor than the caffeine. Fairly quickly, they got back on the road.

At a few minutes after nine o'clock, they arrived at Aunt Vi's two-story, gingerbread Victorian house in the historic district of Leadville. The color scheme of gray, black and lilac qualified this place as a "painted lady" without being too showy—a description that might also apply to the woman who posed on the wide veranda and watched him park in the driveway. Like Daisy, Aunt Violet had streaked blond hair. Unlike Daisy, who usually wore her hair in a tumbledown ponytail, Vi's hair was cut to chin length, straight with bangs. Though Daisy had told him that her aunt was sixty-eight, she could have passed for ten or even twenty years younger.

When Daisy came around the SUV and stood beside him, he said, "Your aunt looks like she belongs in that painted-lady house."

"She's perfected a style that I call classic Western. A tailored shirt tucked into a midcalf, faux-leather skirt and snakeskin cowboy boots. The jewelry is, of course, silver and turquoise." She gave her aunt a good-natured grin and waved. "On some people the outfit would be cliché, but Vi pulls it off."

When Daisy introduced him, Violet gave him a handshake and a perfect smile with precisely applied dark red lipstick. "Should I be worried, Ranger Carter, about my niece not coming home last night?"

"I apologize, ma'am. We got caught up in a serial killer investigation."

Her eyebrows lifted, but she maintained her composure. "Won't you come inside? I should mention that I have another guest. You've met him before, Daisy. Eric Wolff."

Carter scanned the curb in front of the house. His gaze stuck on a dark blue van with the logo for Wolff House Painting and a pyramid of gallon paint cans on the side. Beside him, Daisy growled. "He's not our friend. Eric showed up last night near the murder scene, which makes me think he might have been following me. As a matter of fact, I'm going to ask him right now."

She charged through the front door, leaving him and her aunt on the front porch. If Carter had been in charge of the investigation, he would have reined Daisy in before she physically assaulted a suspect, but he had neither the authority nor the inclination to stop her. Her anger might push Eric into saying something incriminating.

He held the door for Vi. "After you, ma'am."

"I hope you won't mind if I ask a personal question," she said. "Are you married?"

"Not married. Not engaged."

Her red-lipstick smile widened like a Cheshire cat. "Would you like coffee? And a homemade cinnamon scone?"

"Yes, please."

While Vi strode down the central hallway toward what he assumed was the kitchen, he followed the sound of Daisy's voice into a sitting room that was furnished with an eclectic combination of ornate antiques and furniture of many styles and eras. He didn't know much about interior decorating, but he liked this room. It showed personality.

Daisy had positioned herself in front of Eric Wolff, who slouched in a burgundy velvet wing-back chair beside a chrome end table. Her voice hit a stern, authoritative note, reminding him that she was a high school teacher who regularly dealt with cranky adolescents. The age didn't apply to Wolff, who was in his thirties, but the attitude was a fit.

"I'll ask you again," Daisy said, "did you follow me to that campground?"

"You aren't the center of the world, Daisy."

"I think you've been stalking me." She glanced over at Carter. "That's illegal, isn't it?"

"You could file a restraining order compelling Mr. Wolff to stay away from you."

Eric curled his arms tightly against his body. "I didn't do anything wrong."

His shoulder-length blond hair fell around his boyish face in limp, tangled strands. Though he wasn't fat, his cheeks were pudgy, and he had a button nose. From the interview at the campground, Carter knew Eric's age, address in Pueblo and occupation—if he could call being an unemployed housepainter a real job.

"Nice van," Carter said. "Do you take jobs in places other than Pueblo?"

"Sure." His shoulders hunched.

"Ever worked in Glenwood Springs?"

"Yeah. Why?"

"Around the tenth of June, were you in Glenwood?"

His gaze shifted nervously. "I'd have to check my schedule."

Vi entered the room carrying a tray with coffee mugs for Daisy and Carter along with sugar and cream. She placed the tray on a large marble-topped coffee table, and the fresh-roasted aroma wafted pleasantly through the room. Vi straightened. "Daisy, please come to the kitchen with me. I need help carrying the scones."

Carter sat on the long sofa nearest Eric's chair, took off his cowboy hat and picked up his coffee mug. He didn't use cream or sugar, especially not on good, strong coffee like this with subtle undertones of nuts and berries. A far cry from the diner.

He licked his lips and glanced over at Eric. Several possible questions rattled around in Carter's head, but he wasn't sure where to start. The silent treatment had proved effective for him in past interviews. Eric seemed immature and nervous—the sort of man who needed to start talking to fill an uncomfortable silence. He'd say too much rather than too little.

Daisy didn't like him, which was reason enough for Carter to suspect this thirtysomething guy who lived with his father in Pueblo. What was the deal with Eric Wolff? Was he a stalker, too afraid to approach Daisy directly? Or was he a killer?

"Do I need to get a lawyer?" Eric asked.

"Have you done something illegal?"

"Hell, no," he said. "Daisy is the one you ought to be

investigating. She has all kinds of secrets. She and Vi are cheating me and my dad out of millions."

Daisy stalked into the room, carrying another tray with napkins, silverware, clotted cream and two flavors of jam. "You're a liar."

Aunt Vi followed with the scones on a separate plate. "Settle down. Both of you."

Carter wanted to pounce on the cinnamon scones and not listen to their bickering. His cell phone bleeped, indicating a text message coming through, and he grabbed the excuse. "Excuse me, I need to take this." Caller ID showed it was from the FBI.

He went to the front door, opened the screen and stepped onto the porch before tapping on the text. Agent Wiley had identified the blonde he'd found at the boot hill using fingerprints. Her name was Andrea Lindstrom. Why did that sound so familiar? Who was she? The gang partying at the campground hadn't mentioned her.

Carter studied the accompanying photo from her driver's license, and the puzzle pieces clicked into place. He knew her.

He looked away from the image on the screen. Last night, he'd stared down at her ravaged remains in the shallow grave. Half her face had been torn away. The silk scarf at her throat had been encrusted with blood. In his mind, he erased that horrific image. Instead, he remembered a day when he'd talked to this sweet, gentle woman about the tragic death of her dear friend Hannah Guerrero.

Andrea had been reported missing on the fourteenth. Was that timing correct? Hannah was killed on June 10, and Andrea disappeared on June 14. But Daisy had placed time of death for Andrea at two or three days ago, which would have been June 17. Where had she been between the time when she went missing and when she died?

Chapter Six

Still wondering about the link between two of the victims, Carter put away his phone, opened the screen door and stepped back into the house. Standing outside the sitting room, he paused to listen before entering. He didn't hear Daisy yelling or Eric whimpering, which was a good sign, because he didn't want to spend the day on a childish spitting match. Aunt Vi was lecturing them both on the standards of courteous behavior that separated civilized beings from the beasts.

After an apology for slipping out, Carter returned to his seat and broke off a piece of scone, which he slathered with clotted cream and strawberry jam. Daisy sat at the opposite end of the sofa, as far away from Eric as she could get. Her cheeks were flushed with an angry red, her jaw thrust out at a stubborn angle and the line of her soft, sensuous lips had flattened. If Eric was angry, he didn't show it. His shoulders had caved in on his baggy midsection. His mouth trembled, and his watery blue eyes flickered on the verge of tears.

"Thank you, Miss Violet," Eric said, sounding like a child. "I never ever meant to insult you. Or Daisy."

An indecipherable rumble came from Daisy.

Vi gave her a harsh glance. "Did you have something to say, dear? Speak up."

Carter filled his mouth with scone to keep from laughing at Daisy's obvious struggle to control her outrage.

"I'm sorry for raising my voice," Daisy said. "I have a simple question for our guest."

"Go ahead and ask," Aunt Vi said, playing mediator.

"Eric, did you follow me to the campground?"

"No," he said quickly. "You didn't see me following, did you?"

Carter sipped coffee to wash down the scone. He believed Eric. Not because he was innocent, but there were other ways to keep track of another person's whereabouts. Also, he didn't think Eric was capable of following without being noticed. He wasn't a hunter.

"A follow-up," Daisy said. "Did you pay Jackknife to stall until after dark before bringing me to the boot hill?"

He looked down and shrugged. "Not really."

Carter didn't believe him.

"Another question," he said. "Where were you this morning before you came to Leadville?"

"Sleeping. Why?"

"Did you sleep in your van instead of driving all the way home to Pueblo?"

Eric gave a nod. "Nothing wrong with that."

"Think back to dawn." Carter lowered his voice to a soothing, nonthreatening level. "One of the prettiest times of the day, when the skies turn pink and the soft light reflects on the surface of the water. Don't you think so?"

"Yes," he said hesitantly.

"Birds chirping. Waves rippling," Carter said. "So beautiful."

"Yeah."

"Tell me, Eric. Were you at Teacup Lake this morning?"

"Maybe I was." As soon as the words slipped out, he clapped his hand over his mouth as if he could stuff his confession back inside. "Okay, I saw you there. Saw what you were doing."

"You're keeping an eye on Daisy," Carter said. "How are you doing it? A tracking device in her pocket? A locator hooked up to her phone?"

"Who was doing what to whom?" Vi asked.

"You're worse than a stalker." Daisy's lip curled in a snarl. "You've been spying on me."

"Listen, Daisy, all I want is for us to work together. I really need to find the treasure. Me and my dad have a bunch of debt. If we don't get some kind of payoff, we'll lose the house. I'll never have the kind of future I deserve."

"What do you think you deserve?" Carter asked.

"A home with a sweet wife and two kids, girl and boy. And a golden retriever like I had before my mother left us. She took the dog with her. What kind of woman does that?"

He sounded far more upset about losing his pet puppy than having his mother desert the family. In some ways, he seemed normal—pathetic, but normal. In others, he behaved like a creepy stalker.

"Why would I help you?" Daisy asked.

"I have information about the Brighton Bullion that would help your search, and I'll bet there are plenty of things you can tell me."

"Prove it," Daisy said. "Show me one of those letters

to Morris Wolff that you're always bragging about. You said you had several from Sherwood Brighton's wife."

He dug into an inner pocket of his lightweight canvas jacket. "When we find the treasure, we split it right down the middle. Fifty-fifty."

"You get twenty percent," she countered.

"Forty."

"Twenty-five," she said. "Final offer."

He stood and held a folded sheet of paper just out of her grasp. For the first time, Carter realized that Eric might look soft and dumpy, but, under that layer of fat, he was actually above average height and in decent physical condition.

With a cold laugh, he handed her the paper. "It's a copy. When you're done reading it, call me and give me an equally important clue."

With his pug nose in the air, he stomped across the patterned Oriental rug and exited from the house. Daisy bolted to her feet and chased after him. "Wait up," she said. "I want to know how you're tracking me. Did you bug my phone?"

Carter followed her. He couldn't compel Eric to hand over his tracking devices, a fact that he considered a gigantic lapse in the legal system, but he wanted the jerk to realize that he was creating a problem for himself. Standing at the screen door, Carter said, "I'd advise you to cooperate."

"Fine." Eric's lower lip stuck out. "There's a tracker in the change compartment of your wallet."

"How did you put it there?"

"Let's just say that you should watch your purse more carefully. Anyway, you can take it out and pitch it. I won't be able to follow you on my GPS."

Daisy gave him a reluctant nod. "You better not be lying."

"And you better call me. We've got a deal."

When Carter turned back toward the sitting room, Aunt Vi stood in his way. Her small fists were planted on her hips below her Navajo concha belt. In a stern voice, she asked, "What was Eric saying about what he saw at the lake?"

"Eric was spying," he said, hoping to distract her. "It doesn't seem right that those tracking devices you can order online are legal. There ought to be a law against following a person without their permission. If he was a Peeping Tom, I could arrest him."

"I once had a peeper," she said in a whisper. "It was right after I divorced my second husband, and I wasn't accustomed to taking care of myself."

Mission accomplished: he'd diverted her from talking about the kiss. "What did you do?"

"Well, I bought a gun." A sly smile teased the corners of her lips. "The first of many. Thanks to the peeper, I discovered how much I enjoy shooting things."

Carter would definitely keep that in mind. His phone buzzed with another text message from Special Agent Pat Wiley. Both of the boot hill victims had been dosed with knockout drugs. Rene Williams also had a blood alcohol level of 0.13, indicating that she'd continued drinking after she left the party at the campground.

When Daisy came back toward the porch, where he and Vi were standing, she had her wallet in hand and had pulled out the small tracking device, which she threw down on the sidewalk and stomped on. "That's what I think of Eric Wolff."

"Are you sure you destroyed it?" Vi asked. "Should I get my gun?"

Carter couldn't tell if she was joking and decided not to hang around and find out. As he left the veranda, he spoke to Daisy. "I need to make a few phone calls, but I'll be back in an hour or so and we'll drive down to the FBI office in Pueblo so you can give your statement."

"I'll be ready and waiting."

As he strode toward his SUV, he heard Aunt Vi return to the prior topic. "This is the last time I'm going to ask, Daisy. What happened at the lake?"

At the curb, Carter ducked into his car and took off. He wasn't sure where he was headed but knew he needed some space. Any other location was preferable to a relationship discussion with the well-armed Aunt Violet.

MUCH AS DAISY wanted to avoid the topic of her kiss with Carter at the edge of Teacup Lake, she knew Aunt Vi wouldn't give up until she got an answer. "If I tell you, will you drop the subject?"

"Probably not. I need to stay informed about the doings of my niece. Leadville isn't like the big city. People here watch out for each other. And they gossip. Lord, how they gossip!"

Daisy wasn't sure how her behavior reflected on her aunt. After all, she was supposed to be a wicked woman from the big city, and they expected her to have loose morals. Her actions weren't Vi's fault. "Carter and I were kissing."

"I approve." Vi gave a brisk nod. "He seems like a nice young man with a respectable job as a forest ranger.

Your summer visit might have gotten much more exciting."

"Just a kiss. It doesn't mean anything."

"But it could." Vi gave her a friendly little pat on the bottom like a coach sending a new player into the game. "Run along, dear. He's going to be picking you up again in a little while, and you should get ready. Take a shower, wash your hair and put on some makeup."

Muttering under her breath, Daisy climbed the staircase, crossed the landing and went into her bedroom on the second floor. She'd intended to get cleaned up and change clothes. Not to look more seductive but because she expected this day to be long and possibly complicated. After the FBI interview, she hoped to be attending the autopsy, which wasn't an occasion for getting all dolled up, but she wanted to look clean and sanitary.

Uninvited, Aunt Vi stepped into her room. "Maybe you should borrow something attractive. I have a closet full of outfits I've barely worn."

"Believe me, Vi, if I was planning to make a move on Carter—or any other man, for that matter—you'd be the first person I'd consult." Her aunt was something of an expert, having gone through four husbands and innumerable boyfriends. "But there's no way I can have a serious relationship with a guy who lives in the mountains. My work is in the city, and I love my job."

"Don't be so quick to say no."

Daisy changed the topic. "I found something in Butcher's Gulch. There was a gravestone for Annie Brighton, Sherwood's wife."

"A clue," Vi said with evident delight. "Jackknife said he saw a marker for Brighton, but I wasn't sure whether I could believe him or not. He should have mentioned it was Annie."

"He wanted to impress you. Wants you to date him and fall in love because you're rich and can take care of him."

"But I'm not a wealthy woman," she protested. "And if I were, I most certainly wouldn't be interested in the likes of Jackknife Jones. I have better taste."

"I don't have a lot of information about Annie. Can you give me the highlights?"

"She and Sherwood had three children, and she basically raised them by herself. His career as an outlaw kept him away from home for days at a time." Vi referred to his supposed "career" as though he'd been a busy stockbroker. "He provided for his family, and nobody ever asked where her money came from."

"Maybe because they were scared," Daisy said under her breath.

"You have no call to bad-mouth your ancestor. From all accounts, he was a gentleman."

Except when he was robbing banks. Her proper aunt was quick to turn a blind eye when it came to the treasure. "Go on."

"Annie worked as a seamstress and was acclaimed for making fancy wedding dresses. She lived in Cripple Creek and Pueblo for most of her life."

"But was buried in Butcher's Gulch."

"Tell me more about the headstone," Vi said eagerly. "What did it say?"

"'Annie Brighton. Wife, Friend and Lover.'"

"Aw, that's so sweet. Sherwood still thought of her as his lover." She frowned. "But it doesn't make sense. I seem to remember that he died before she did."

"Maybe one of the kids was responsible for her marker."

Daisy was curious. Why was Annie buried in a boot hill cemetery, which was the final resting place for outlaws and the indigent? She seemed to be a decent woman who made wedding gowns. Why Butcher's Gulch? Who erected her tombstone? Instead of diving into the shower and washing her hair, Daisy sat on the edge of her bed and unfolded the piece of paper Eric had given her. There might be relevant clues in this copy of a letter—dated June 6, 1889—from Annie to Morris Wolff.

Vi sat beside her, reading over her shoulder. "That's two years after the theft of Brighton's Bullion. When I think about it, I'm certain that Sherwood died in 1896, nine years after the big robbery. What was the date on Annie's tombstone?"

"There wasn't one. No date of birth or death."

"Not completely uncommon," Vi said. "Some ladies are rather particular about revealing their age, even after they're dead."

Silently, Daisy read the first few lines, which were carefully written with perfect penmanship. Then she looked up, wide-eyed and surprised. "This is hot stuff. I guess Annie B. didn't like to waste time on foreplay."

"Those descriptions are based on references from the Bible," Vi said. "Her breasts are ripe fruit, firm and juicy. Made for his delight. Could be Song of Solomon."

Annie continued with an imaginative description of Morris Wolff's private parts, which were—supposedly—as hard as oak and hung to his knees. This letter was an 1800's version of the current trend to send naked, obscene photos via text message. Annie couldn't wait until they were "joined together from top to toe" and she could "taste every sweet bite of his quivering flesh."

"Yuck," Daisy said. "I guess we know why her gravestone mentioned that she was a lover, not necessarily with her husband."

Vi pointed to the end of the letter. "This is the only place she even mentions him."

Daisy read aloud. "'Sherwood will never know where I've put the bullion. It's mine now.'"

"Those are the words of an angry woman." Violet shuddered. "We might have been researching the wrong person. Annie seems to be in charge."

"And has possession of the gold."

Daisy had to admit that Eric Wolff had shown them a telling clue for their treasure hunt. She wondered what else he might be hiding.

Chapter Seven

With the windows down, Carter drove through Leadville, one of his favorite little towns, which was part of the territory he regularly patrolled. As he left the outskirts, the late-morning sky stretched wide and blue above him. He needed this space to clear his head. While driving to a rocky hillside he'd visited before, Carter allowed the mountains to nurture his mind and his spirit.

At an elevation over ten thousand feet, Leadville—the highest incorporated town in North America—boomed into existence during the 1889 silver rush, but the real treasure was the beauty of the surroundings. Nine fourteeners, including Mount Elbert and the aptly named Mount Massive, dominated the landscape. Carter thought these peaks, still snowcapped in the latter half of June, might have provided inspiration for the explorer who saw this mountain range at dawn when the sun had painted the snow a bright red. *Sangre de Cristo* meant "blood of Christ."

Leaving the main road, he guided his NPS vehicle to a clearing at the top of a rise with a heavy-duty picnic table and benches that had seen better days. He swung open the car door, stepped into the sunshine and inhaled the scent of resin, dust and pine cones. Though he had a desk and computer at the NPS headquarters in Salida, he considered places like this—with soul-stirring views of high peaks and abundant forests—to be his office. He'd never trade this job for a cubicle.

Wishing he'd brought a thermos of Aunt Vi's excellent coffee, he stepped onto the bench, sat on the tabletop, took off his cowboy hat and welcomed the breeze that ruffled his hair. He looked to the mountains for answers. One side of his brain popped with questions about the serial killer investigation, while the other was preoccupied with Daisy. From the moment they met, he'd liked her. He admired her smart analysis of the victims' remains. The bubbling sound of her laughter made him smile. He'd never forget the way her lips tasted when they kissed.

He stared across the foothills to the rugged mountains beyond. What the hell was he going to do? The answer came fast—first, he had to stop the serial killer.

And he needed expert advice. Using the sat phone with a strong signal, he called Joaquin Stanley. His supervisor, a former hippie, brought a unique set of skills to his work. He had degrees in forestry, environmental biology and psychology. Before joining the Park Service, he'd been a farmer, a firefighter and a therapist/counselor who specialized in the treatment of perpetrators. His analysis of the serial killer's motives would provide a solid profile.

When Joaquin answered, Carter gave him a quick rundown of the progress on the investigation, including the important fact that the FBI in Pueblo had taken over jurisdiction. "The special agent in charge is SAC Pat Wiley. I've worked with him before."

"Sounds like you've got everything covered. Why are you calling me?"

"I could use your help in profiling the killer," Carter said.

"Stop by this afternoon."

"Can't. I've got an appointment at the FBI office in Pueblo. Then I'm going to watch the autopsy."

"You?" Joaquin questioned. "You've never liked the gory part of the job."

"Yeah, well, people change."

"I'm sensing something from you. What's going on?"

"Nothing." Carter knew his supervisor well. He imagined the burly man stroking his neatly trimmed, salt-and-pepper beard, a remnant of the ZZ Top look he wore in his hippie days. "I don't know what you're talking about."

"There's definite change. You're not acting like a lonesome cowboy anymore."

"Never was a cowboy." Living in the wilderness suited him, but he hadn't grown up on a ranch and didn't ride the range. Bouncing around on a horse gave him a stiff back and an achy ass.

"You know what I mean," Joaquin said. "It's your attitude, your independent nature. You're like Gary Cooper or Clint Eastwood—a kickass loner taming the Wild West."

That description fit a lot of rangers and mountain men. "If I'm a cowboy, what are you?"

"Lumberjack," he said proudly. "My ex-wife used to like watching me chop wood. No kidding. She said it made her horny."

Though he'd come to Joaquin for his expert opinion,

Carter enjoyed their wide-ranging conversations. "As long as we're talking about women…"

"Aha!" Carter heard Joaquin slam the flat of his large hand against his desktop. "I know what's different about you. You're in love. Well, good luck to you, Ranger. It's about time."

"I'm not saying you're right, but suppose I met a strong, stubborn woman who loves her life in the city and will never move to the mountains. How do I change her mind?"

"Never start a relationship thinking you can change the other person. Either you accept her as she is or you quit your job and move into town."

"You're saying it's up to me. I'm the one who has to change."

"Not necessarily. You and your lady friend can hook up for a couple of days and then go your separate ways."

A quick affair wasn't what Carter wanted. With Daisy, something more was possible—something amazing. He'd tried marriage before, and it had lasted less than two years. He wasn't good at being half of a couple. His ex-wife called him a loner. But Daisy was independent and strong and unlike any other woman he'd met. A relationship with her would be an adventure.

His gaze lifted to the vast panorama of the Sangre de Cristos. This was his home. He never wanted to live anywhere else. If she didn't change her mind…

"Profiling." He switched gears. This phone call was, after all, about the serial killer. "Here's what I can tell you about the three victims. They were all young and pretty. All were found in graveyards but might not have been killed there. Long silk scarves were tied around the fatal wounds to their throats. Two of them—Hannah and Andrea—knew each other."

"What's different about the three victims?" Joaquin asked.

"Different physical types. Hannah had black hair, dark eyes and a muscular frame. Andrea was a willowy blonde, pale skinned, not an outdoors type. And Rene Williams, the most recent victim, had long brown hair and she was petite."

"What else?"

"Different occupations. Hannah was a dental assistant. Andrea worked for an insurance company. They both lived in the Glenwood Springs area in apartments. Didn't have roommates. Rene was a college student from Denver who had just broken up with a live-in boyfriend."

"How about the times of death? When were they killed?"

"I can't be precise until after the autopsies, but Daisy made a couple of good guesses about when the women in Butcher's Gulch were killed."

"Daisy," Joaquin said. "Is she a coroner? A medical examiner?"

"A high school biology teacher from Denver." He kept his voice level to avoid betraying his feelings for her. "She teaches anatomy and studied forensic medicine at a body farm."

"And she gave you an expert opinion?"

"That's right. Records show that Hannah was murdered on June 10. Andrea was probably killed on June 17 but went missing on the fourteenth. Rene died last night, on June 20."

"First victim on the tenth, second on the seventeenth,

third on the twentieth." Joaquin exhaled with a whoosh. "I can see why you need a profile ASAP. The shorter periods between kills could be an indication that he's planning another murder very soon."

"We need to act fast."

Carter heard the scrape of a chair being pushed back from a desk. He knew Joaquin was on his feet, pacing across the black-and-sienna-patterned Navajo area rug in his office. Part of his process was moving. He said physical activity jogged his brain. "When you found the bodies, what was your first impression?"

"Hannah and Rene were arranged to look like they were asleep, but Andrea's body had been mauled by predators." He thought of Daisy's suggestion that the killer had tried to shield the body. "He might have tried to protect Andrea with some kind of covering."

"Tell me about these scarves."

Carter imagined his supervisor standing at the window of his office, looking out at the Collegiate Peaks—Mount Princeton, Mount Harvard and so on. "The scarves are similar and were put on after death. I'm thinking the killer brought them with him."

"Did you find a murder weapon?"

"No." Carter shook his head. "The autopsy will tell us about the two in Butcher's Gulch. Hannah's throat was slashed by a heavy-duty hunting knife."

"Doesn't exactly narrow it down," Joaquin complained. "Sexual assault?"

"Not on Hannah. We have to wait for the autopsy to know about the other two. My gut tells me no." He described the way Rene's hair was styled and her blouse buttoned up to the collar. "So, what should I look for? I'm hoping you can be more specific than the usual parameters for a serial killer—white male between twenty-eight and forty-five. Abusive childhood. Egocentric with lack of remorse."

"An organized killer," Joaquin said. "He planned ahead, bringing a weapon and a special scarf. It's possible that his planning extends to the selection of his victims. He might get a thrill from learning her habits, might watch her or follow her."

"A stalker."

Carter thought of Eric Wolff and the tracking device he'd planted on Daisy. Though it seemed coincidental that Eric's interest in treasure hunting meshed with serial murders, he might be clever enough to hide one by focusing on the other. It ought to be easy enough to check Eric's whereabouts on the night Hannah was killed.

Joaquin added, "If he grabbed Andrea and held her for three days before killing her, he might have been playing house with her. Following some kind of fantasy."

Or hurting her. He remembered ligature marks on the wrists. If the killer took captives, he needed a private place to hold them. "He didn't do that for Hannah. Or for Rene."

"He might have bonded with them. You know, singing a song together or dancing. He found ways to stay close to his victims that wouldn't make sense to anyone else."

Like Jackknife Jones driving Daisy in circles. "What else?"

"His motivations are complex," Joaquin said. "I'd be surprised to learn he's driven by a sexual fantasy. Instead, look for a psychologically unhealthy connection to his mother, sister or another close family member. A trigger incident with one of those women might jolt him into the need to commit murder. It's like he's rescuing them by killing them."

"What kind of incident?"

"Triggers might involve a death, a divorce, an argument or a separation. Mom might have divorced Dad and started a new family. The son would see murder as a way to keep Mom close."

"By killing other women?"

"There's a good deal of rage braided into his sadness and/or grief."

A twisted way of thinking. "What makes you study these perpetrators? What's the appeal in forensic psychology?"

"Maybe you should ask your new girlfriend, the biology teacher, why she studies corpses." Joaquin chuckled. "Call me after you have some results from the autopsy. I'll be interested in hearing about this investigation. And in meeting Daisy."

"Not that you've figured out who she is, what should I do about her?"

"Try chopping wood."

WHEN DAISY SLIPPED into the passenger seat of the NPS vehicle, she realized that her khaki skirt—a loose-fitting A-line—displayed a lot of leg, probably her best feature in the summer when she had a natural tan. She glanced over at Carter behind the steering wheel, tempted to explain that she'd chosen a skirt for her FBI interview so she'd look respectable, but then she'd also have to justify the black V-neck T-shirt that clung to her breasts under her lightweight brown jacket. Though she wasn't trying to look seductive, her outfit told a different story. Was she subconsciously putting out signals? Why else would she have blow-dried her curly blond hair into a smooth style that swooped gracefully across her forehead?

This was *not* a date. They'd drive to Pueblo, where she'd have an interview with the FBI and observe an autopsy. She had two other graveyards she wanted to check out as long as they were in the area. *Nothing romantic about any of those plans.*

Leaning back in her seat, she gazed through the windshield at a verdant June day with fluffy white clouds skipping across an azure sky. Fresh grasses dotted with crimson and blue wildflowers blanketed the valley below jagged red cliffs. The Arkansas River, flush with runoff from melted snow, cascaded beside the highway. On a day like this, when the late-morning breeze smelled like summer and sun, she easily understood why Carter loved living in the mountains instead of being a cop on the hot, dry, city streets of Denver.

She exhaled a quiet sigh. If they hadn't been hunting a serial killer, the day would have been perfect. "What did your profiler say about the crimes?"

"He has a theory based on the way the killer grooms and cares for the victims. It's almost as if he has an attachment to them."

"Then why would he kill them?"

"I talked to my supervisor about that. I'll tell you later." His eyebrows lowered in a scowl. "There was another issue with Andrea. According to SAC Wiley, she was reported missing on the fourteenth, but you placed time of death on the seventeenth or eighteenth. Where was she during those missing days?"

Daisy shuddered to think of the platinum blonde being held captive by the serial killer, especially since Andrea had known what had happened to her friend Hannah. Her body had been too mangled by predators to pinpoint signs of abuse, but there were ligature marks on her wrists and arms. "From her wounds, I can't tell if he hurt her…" She hesitated to use the word *torture*. "I didn't see scars or bruises indicating that he injured Rene. From what you told me about Hannah, her death came swiftly."

"Joaquin—my NPS Supervisor who used to be a psychologist—suggested that these weren't random killings. He stalks, pursues and captures women who have some kind of connection to him. Possibly he imagines affection—something he might feel for a family member, maybe even his mother." Carter groped for words to explain. "He might be using his victims as surrogates for women he felt close to. He might talk to them or sing to them."

Not surprisingly, the motivation for this serial killer also mystified her. Why would he do these terrible, degrading things? How could he think playing with his captives meant he cared for them? "I'm not great at putting myself into somebody else's head."

"Not when their thinking is so warped."

"But your supervisor knows forensic psychology. He studies perpetrators. What does that say about him?"

"I might ask the same of you. Why do you study dead people?" He gazed into her eyes, making a quick but deep connection. "For that matter, I must be as weird as you and Joaquin, because I like talking to both of you."

She continued to stare after he looked back at the road. In spite of herself, she wondered if he'd noticed how mascara brought out the green in her eyes. "Do you think I'm weird?"

"Not weird. I think you're extraordinary."

Definitely a first. No one had ever said that to her before. Uncomfortable, she wanted to get back to the business of investigating. "How can we use this profile?"

"When we're considering suspects, we should look for triggers—incidents involving his mother or a woman he was close to. What can you tell me about Eric Wolff?"

"He's not a killer," she protested. "He's a jealous, small-minded treasure hunter."

"He fits some parameters for the killer. He's the right age, has a job with flexible hours and can easily transport bodies in his van. He admitted to stalking you."

Every word he spoke rang true. She'd been disturbed when Eric confessed that he'd watched when Carter kissed her. Definitely a creep. But a serial killer?

"He lives in Pueblo with his father," she said. "His mother isn't in the picture. I think she left them when Eric was a teenager."

"Could be a trigger."

"But it happened a long time ago. Eric's in his thirties. Surely he's had time to get over being abandoned so many years ago."

"Some people never do. Early abandonment can scar a person for life."

"True." Her own upbringing as the only child of older parents had been relatively stable and free from tragedy. Not for the first time, she was thankful for being average. "What we should be asking is why now? What would activate Eric's early trauma?"

"We'll have to research his mother. She might be

getting married to someone other than his father. Or she might have died."

"There's an easy way to verify if he was the killer or not," she said. "Check his alibi. Was he in Glenwood Springs when Hannah was killed? Or was that unverified?"

His mouth twisted in a wry grin. "I know why you're an anatomy whiz, but how do you know about alibis?"

"I read suspense novels," she said.

"Hannah was hanging out at a tavern with friends, including Andrea, and told them she was going to meet a guy who wanted to see the memorial to Doc Holliday. Could Eric pull that off?"

Slowly, she nodded. An awareness of danger spread through her. Her skin prickled. The first time she met Eric, he made a point of talking to her about cemeteries and the boot hill graveyards. He had convinced Aunt Vi to start looking for Sherwood Brighton's grave. Was Eric the killer?

A seed of fear had been planted in the back of her mind. During the two-and-a-half-hour drive, they discussed other suspects—including Slade Franklin, who also lived in Pueblo and was someone they'd visit while there. But she couldn't dismiss the thought of Eric Wolff stalking her through the forest.

When they got to the outskirts of Pueblo, she saw a dark blue van on the other side of the street, too far for her to make out the features of the driver. He drove out of sight before she could read the logo and see the image of paint cans. Was it him? Walking on the sidewalk, she saw a man who shuffled like Eric. This was his hometown. He could be anywhere. Waiting. Watching. Planning his attack.

Chapter Eight

The headquarters for the Pueblo branch of the FBI spread across the eighth and ninth floors of an office building around the corner from the Pueblo County Detention Center and the county sheriff's office. Daisy should have felt safe within these orderly corridors where cubicles and clusters of desks for field agents occupied open spaces and partitioned private offices lined the inner walls. Though these lawmen and women had locked their weapons away while in the office, they were equipped with the skill and training to protect her. Certainly they looked professional—most of the agents wore slacks and tucked-in shirts with blazers. Several had neckties.

A red-haired agent she recognized from the boot hill approached them and slapped Carter on the back in an aggressively friendly gesture. The agent was average height, but he appeared to be bigger due to the biceps bulging inside his shirtsleeves, giving the impression that if he flexed the seams would split. His striped necktie draped over his pecs and pointed toward his muscular thighs. When he shook Daisy's hand, she braced for a mighty grip and wasn't disappointed. She gritted her teeth to keep from flinching.

"Not sure we met at Butcher's Gulch," he said. "I'm Special Agent Mickey Hicks."

The guy with the cartoon character name. "I'm Daisy Brighton. Please call me Daisy."

"Sorry you got mixed up in this, Daisy, but don't you worry. We'll nab this guy."

She'd come here as a witness to give a statement, but Hicks's pale blue eyes seemed to accuse her. A sensation of undeserved guilt prickled across her skin like goose bumps. She hadn't done anything wrong but couldn't help but worry that some long-forgotten infraction would rise up and point an accusing finger in her direction.

Carter reintroduced her to SAC Pat Wiley, who was the opposite of Hicks. While Hicks was hard-edged and intense, Wiley reminded her of a pair of well-worn loafers—not pretty but exceedingly comfortable. He was average-looking with thinning brown hair, an easy grin and a bolo tie fastened with a circular silver slide etched with a howling coyote. *A wily coyote? Another cartoon?* His handshake reassured her, and so did his compliment—"Your analysis of the time of death seems to be right on target. We appreciate your assistance."

"I'm glad. But how did that help?"

"In the early part of the investigation, we gather as much information as possible on the actual crime. Your observations of insect larvae and the development of maggots caused you to place the time of death for these women at least two days apart. A significant detail."

A woman in a white lab coat, obviously a forensic investigator, picked her way through the desks and handed a folder to Hicks. Her tone was crisp. "DNA results confirm the identity of Rene Williams. By the way, you're welcome for the rush analysis."

Before Wiley could comment, she pivoted and left. Wiley ushered her and Carter into a small interrogation room with a table, four chairs and a two-way mirror on one wall. The space looked exactly as she expected from watching TV cop shows. Wiley gestured for her and Carter to sit on one side of the table while he took a chair opposite them, opened a fat envelope and took out a folder with forms, papers and photographs inside.

For a few moments, Carter and Wiley lobbed ideas back and forth, much the way she and Carter had on the drive. As far as she was concerned, this was unnecessary talk. The autopsy would provide information about whether the victim been restrained, raped or tortured. Carter opened a new direction to their speculation, asking about where Andrea might have been held. Did the killer live in the Glenwood Springs area where he'd met Andrea and Hannah? Or was Butcher's Gulch closer to his home base? Or was it totally unrelated to the victims? He might live in Pueblo.

Daisy lacked the ability to judge distances in the mountains, which was why Jackknife had managed to drive her in circles. When the GPS on her phone went on the fritz, she was well and truly lost. The vast distances between towns and other areas heightened her respect for Carter's job. He didn't have as many violent crimes to investigate as a city cop, but his jurisdiction covered a wide and varied topography. Looking to Wiley, he said, "No matter where he lives, we'll need warrants to get your forensic investigators inside his truck or van."

"As soon as you give me cause, I'm on it." Wiley

turned his head and pinned Daisy with a surprisingly sharp gaze. She figured he was deciding whether or not he should talk about the crime in her presence. "You might be more comfortable in the waiting room, Ms. Brighton."

"It's Daisy," she said. "And I don't mind hearing about your investigation."

"Having her observe is unorthodox," Carter said, "but she could be useful. The medical examiner has already agreed to let her attend the autopsies this afternoon."

"I'm impressed." Wiley arched an eyebrow. "Dr. Julia Stillwater doesn't break the rules for just anybody."

"Plus, Daisy is connected with two of the suspects—Jackknife Jones and Eric Wolff."

"Very well." Wiley adjusted his bolo tie and consulted a report from his folder. "I have information from the Glenwood Springs PD. They initiated their investigation into Andrea Lindstrom's disappearance after receiving a call from the insurance office where she worked. Her apartment showed no signs of being broken into. None of her friends or family had heard from her. The Glenwood cops were thorough. They didn't find any leads."

Daisy absorbed his words. Was Andrea grabbed off the street? Did the killer invite her to have a cup of coffee with him? Unlikely! No way would she engage in casual conversation with a stranger after what had happened to her friend Hannah. "I wonder if she drove home after work on the day before she went missing. Where was her car?"

"In a grocery store parking lot."

A clear picture formed in her mind. "I'll bet her shopping bags were half loaded into the trunk."

"Good hunch," Wiley said. "How did you know that?"

"I'm a single woman who tries to be cautious. When I get out of my car, I hold the vial of pepper spray on my key chain, cocked and ready to fire. I don't even think about the pepper spray anymore. It's habit." Though not aware of being nervous, her voice cracked. She cleared her throat. "I'm most vulnerable when I'm in the middle of unloading stuff and my arms are full."

Under the table, Carter took her hand and gently squeezed. She hoped he didn't feel her trembling.

"Good reasoning," Wiley said. "That's pretty much what the Glenwood cops concluded."

"I liked working with those detectives," Carter said. "What else did they find?"

"Hannah Guerrero had a connection with Pueblo. Her great-uncle died in October of last year, and she attended the funeral at Rolling Hills Cemetery."

Daisy's ears pricked up. That cemetery was on her list of places where Sherwood Brighton could be buried. "Where is that located?"

"South Pueblo. I can give you directions." He flipped a page in his folder. "That evening, she went jogging along the Riverwalk."

The few bits of information she recalled about Hannah included her occupation as a dental assistant and her high level of physical fitness. An evening jog made sense, and the Riverwalk was a charming location where the wide Arkansas River curled through the center of town. Elegantly landscaped, the sprawling acreage housed a selection of shops and restaurants. The renovations represented an integral part of Pueblo's transformation from the so-called Steel City to an artsy community with galleries, concerts and a ballet company.

"On that very same night," Wiley said, "the body of a young woman was found among the trees at the north edge of the Riverwalk. Not a well-lighted area, but she was visible from the sidewalk where Hannah and other joggers would have been running. The victim had been arranged with her back against a thick tree trunk. At first, an observer might think she was taking a break from her stroll and resting while she peacefully watched the river roll by."

"How cold was it?" Daisy asked.

"In early evening, around fifty or fifty-five. The victim wore a light jacket and jeans."

He took an eight-by-ten photo from the folder and slid it across the table to Carter, who shared the picture with her. Daisy agreed with Wiley's statement about the victim appearing to be resting. His next photo showed heavy bruising around her throat. *Strangled.*

The method of killing differed from the three women in the current investigation, but the way the body had been arranged echoed the Butcher's Gulch murderer's careful display of his victims. She wasn't an expert on criminal behavior, but the appearance of another dead woman who was connected with Hannah had to be more than coincidence. "Did Hannah find the body?"

"She didn't report it but was definitely in the area."

Though she and Carter had discovered the most recent victims, the roots of these serial killings stretched back farther into the past. Could there have been others? How many? She imagined an endless queue of young women clutching their throats with their eyes closed in death and their mouths gaping open in silent screams.

Goose bumps broke out on her arms. She might already have met this killer, might have heard his voice and inhaled the smell of bloodlust clinging to him. Would she know him when he came close? Or would he blend in, indistinguishable until he attacked?

Her chills solidified in a frozen lump in her chest, making it hard to breathe. She groped for Carter's hand, needing his strength and reassurance, but he was leaning across the table toward Wiley, his gaze intense. His voice took on an avid tone. "Is it unusual for a serial killer to change his method of murder?"

"It happens." Wiley shrugged. "He's still defining himself."

"What about the scarf?" Carter asked. "The woman on the Riverwalk wasn't wearing a scarf."

A photograph of a silver necklace with a heart pendant joined the other two pictures on the table. "None of her friends or family recognized the necklace she was wearing. He crushed her throat with so much force that the chain embedded in her skin. A reenactment of the crime based on forensic evidence indicated that he stood behind her, perhaps fastening the heart necklace at her nape before he choked her."

"Strangulation is nowhere near as messy as a slicing an artery and seems less efficient," Carter said. "Why change?"

"We can agree that he's an organized killer who plans every detail and doesn't leave much to chance. Strangling might seem tidy, but a victim who's being choked is more likely to fight."

"Not if he grabs them from behind," Carter said.

"She might kick, might throw herself on the ground or break away and cry for help."

Daisy felt the blood drain from her face. Studying the deceased didn't bother her but hearing about the struggle before death set her imagination racing down a dark, dangerous pathway. She seldom went to horror movies. And when the scary music started playing, she covered her eyes and gritted her teeth so she wouldn't scream. "Are there others? How long has he been killing?"

"I'm waiting to get more information," Wiley said. "The Riverwalk victim came from the Southern Ute Reservation near Durango. The investigation was taken over by tribal police."

Carter nodded. "I've never had a problem dealing with the tribes."

"That's because you're a ranger, a protector of the forests. They don't see you as the enemy. You'd be surprised by how many people resent the FBI and don't want to cooperate."

Daisy understood that reluctance. Moments ago, when she entered the offices of the all-powerful FBI, she'd been nervous, expecting to be arrested for a forgotten crime, something so minor that she didn't remember. The tribal police had reason to distrust the feds, stemming from a history of broken treaties and land grabs. She could understand why they'd prefer to work with an investigative ranger like Carter who shared their respect for the land.

"In any case," Wiley said, "we're expanding our computer search to include young women who were missing or killed in the past ten years."

An endless line of victims... Unable to cope with the idea of so much fear—terror from the murdered women who knew they were about to die and from her own deep-seated nightmares—Daisy went silent while Carter and Wiley continued to discuss the investigation.

In her imagination, the murderer evolved into a monster with blood dripping from his fangs and his fingernails sharpened into talons. *Ridiculous.* According to science, the natural world contained many horrifying creatures, including the apex predators at the top of the food chain. Great white sharks, Burmese pythons and grizzlies were virtual killing machines. Horrifying and lethal but predictable, they didn't frighten her as much as an innocent-looking individual who lured his prey into danger. She wanted this serial killer caught. At the same time, she realized there wasn't much she could do to find and arrest a murderer. Daisy hadn't trained as an investigator.

As soon as they were done at the FBI office, she and Carter would observe the autopsy. A much better use of her skills.

Chapter Nine

As they approached the autopsy suite, Carter trained his watchful gaze on Daisy. In her short skirt with her practical hiking boots, her tanned legs provided a sexy distraction from his concerns about her state of mind. She'd told him repeatedly that she was fine. Her posture and athletic gait showed the confidence he'd come to expect from her. But when she reached up and brushed a shiny wing of blond hair off her forehead, she avoided looking at him. She'd been jumpy since they left Leadville. During their time with SAC Wiley in the interrogation room, her nervousness had increased. The roses in her cheeks faded to ash. Her hands trembled.

He didn't understand. He'd watched this woman calmly examine maggots on a corpse and lean close to check the wounds. But talking about the investigation had her rattled. When they got down to the official business of Wiley taking her witness statement for the record, she'd regained some of her poise, especially when she discussed the injuries on the victims.

What's she hiding? Every time he asked if she was okay, she said the same thing: "Fine." He didn't think she was lying. Why would she? But there was definitely something she wasn't telling him.

He paused outside the autopsy area and asked, "Are you sure you want to do this?"

"I've been looking forward to watching Dr. Julia Stillwater work." When she gazed up at him, her green eyes widened. Her smile seemed genuine. "She's a legend. According to one of my former profs, there's nobody better than Dr. Stillwater. She's done tremendous work on facial reconstruction."

Though he believed her enthusiasm, he still saw tension. "Maybe we should grab a cup of coffee before we go inside."

"I'd rather watch."

Actually, he wouldn't mind another coffee. Last night, he hadn't slept, and it was almost lunchtime. "Are you hungry?"

"I'm fine."

Fine. He was beginning to hate that word. Because she wasn't fine. She was frightened, on edge. "Something's bothering you, and I want to know what it is."

"Nothing, really."

He had no choice but to follow her into a carpeted waiting area with its functional chairs and tables. The boring furniture was where the resemblance to other institutional settings ended. An abstract painting of the high desert landscape covered the walls in turquoise, gold, sienna and purple—colors associated with the Southwest. Leafy plants, like dieffenbachia, dragon tree and that one with the spidery leaves, ranged around the room in terra cotta pots, also painted with colorful geometric designs. A sign that said Autopsy marked the wall beside a windowed door. On the opposite side was the forensic laboratory. Haunting melodies from a wooden flute shimmered in the background.

"Mellow." Daisy's tension took a giant step toward calm. "This decor has got to be from the earth mother influence of Julia Stillwater."

He'd only met the doctor in person once before and had never attended an autopsy, but he respected her knowledge and had immediately liked this strong Ute tribal elder who supervised a clinic on the reservation in addition to her work as a medical examiner.

In the anteroom outside the large area where the actual autopsies would be performed, an intern in scrubs wearing a Harley-Davidson surgical cap and a black N95 mask took their names and directed them to the area where they could change into hats, booties, gloves, masks and disposable suits to cover their clothes.

While she got dressed in the sanitary gear, Daisy asked, "Have they started the autopsy?"

"They're still doing the external exam." The intern shrugged. "What's the deal with these victims? There's a whole bunch of observers."

Carter expected as much. There would be agents from the FBI, state police and the coroner for Pueblo County, at the very least. "It's a possible serial killer."

The intern's dark brown eyes were his only visible feature. He squeezed them closed and then open, an expression that could have meant surprise, excitement or just about anything else. "Whoa."

"Has the autopsy uncovered any forensic data, like a tox screen?"

"There was one done, but I don't have the details." He bobbed his head. "The only thing Doc Julia said was that the suggested time of death was within reasonable parameters."

Daisy nudged his arm. "Did you hear that? I'm within reasonable parameters."

They entered the autopsy room, where two stainless steel tables with gutters on either side were set up in the midst of other equipment, including measuring devices, scalpels, forceps, shears, saws and other tools he didn't recognize. Dr. Julia Stillwater turned the naked body of Rene Williams onto her side to display the dark purpling of lividity on her back and torso. One intern held the body in place while another took photos.

Behind her plastic face shield, the doctor wore a recording microphone headset. She motioned to the intern with the camera and pointed to the grayish flesh of Rene's arm. "Butterfly tattoo above the ligature marks on her left wrist. Where there's one, often there are more."

With the intern snapping photos, they recorded five other tats, including a horoscope sign for Scorpio and an arrangement of stars that looked like the Big Dipper. Carter looked away from the dead woman. Instead, he focused on the doctor as she moved in a methodical manner from the top of Rene's head to her feet, from her fingertips to her shoulders. Once again, they turned her onto her stomach. With precision, the doctor and her interns recorded all the visible scratches, bruises and wounds.

"Make sure you get a photo of that double puncture," she said, indicating an area on the victim's side. "Those marks either came from a stun gun or she was attacked by a vampire."

The investigators, including Carter, focused on this new revelation. He was fairly sure that Hannah hadn't been hit by a stun gun, which meant the killer had made another change in his procedure. Had he also zapped Andrea?

On Rene's upper back above the shoulder blade, Dr. Stillwater found the final tattoo. The name *Josh* surrounded by a heart. Josh Santana was the boyfriend. Another suspect.

Glancing around the room, Carter counted seven other observers. None were as keenly interested as Daisy, who kept inching closer to the examination table for a better look. When the intern who had been taking photos stepped back, the doctor picked up her scalpel. The overhead surgical lights flashed against the silver blade. The time had come for the Y-shaped incision that would lay the organs bare. Not Carter's idea of a good time.

Behind her plastic face shield, Julia Stillwater grinned at Daisy. "Are you Ms. Brighton?"

"It's an honor to meet you, Doctor."

"You're a biology teacher."

"That's right."

"Good job estimating time of death. We should talk."

"I'd like that."

Carter couldn't see Daisy's mouth behind her mask, but he knew she was smiling from ear to ear. The doctor ranked high in her estimation, and the mere thought of a chat about forensic medicine had wiped away her fears and nervousness. She'd recalibrated her mood. Now, she was really and truly, actually *fine*.

On the other hand, he wasn't altogether thrilled to be here. To be sure, he wanted and needed the forensic evidence that would be revealed when Dr. Stillwater cracked open the rib cage and cut through Rene Williams's breastbone. The doc would discover all kinds of useful details when she removed the major organs and analyzed them. Ditto for the brain.

But he really wasn't interested in the procedure. He didn't care how she reached her conclusions, didn't need to see or smell the actual stomach contents. It was enough for him to read the autopsy report and learn what Rene had eaten for her last meal.

While he searched his mind for a plausible excuse to leave the autopsy, Dr. Stillwater saved him the trouble. She returned her scalpel to the sanitary tray and stepped back from the table. "I think I'll take a break now. Half an hour or so. For those of you who are observing, don't touch the body. Feel free to visit the cafeteria for coffee or tea. Remember to suit up again when you return. Daisy, please come with me."

When she turned and strode from the room, her interns carefully covered the naked body and the surgical tools. Daisy hurried out the door and down the hallway after her idol, and Carter followed.

DAISY'S EXPECTATIONS FOR the office of an earth mother who was also a scientist were happily met when they entered a large room with two tall windows. Long wooden planter boxes filled with basil, peas and peppers stretched beneath each window and were bathed in sunlight. Tendrils of ivy dripped over the edges and touched the floor. In the corner, a big-leafed bird-of-paradise plant reached all the way to the ceiling. A set of bookshelves held intricately painted bowls and vases from the Ute Mountain pottery collection as well as woven baskets. Family photos and artwork done by grandchildren decorated the walls. A casual clutter of papers, folders and books kept the place from looking like a museum.

A small desk—stacked with incoming work—lurked in the corner, while a long, polished walnut table surrounded by comfortable chairs dominated the center of the room. Dr. Stillwater peeled off her protective gear, revealing turquoise scrubs and two long black braids that had been tucked inside her cap. She went to another table and filled the reservoir in a coffee maker with distilled water. "You'll both have coffee," she said. "Feel free to take off the gowns, gloves and masks."

As Carter stripped off the outer layer of sanitary clothing, he thanked her for her hospitality. "We've met before," he said.

"I remember you, Ranger. It's Aloysius Periwinkle Carter, isn't it?"

Aloysius Periwinkle? Daisy squelched the urge to poke fun. She'd been teased about her name that seemed to rhyme with everything, including crazy, lazy and—worst of all—easy.

"A. P. Carter IV." A sheepish grin curled his lips. "You have a good memory."

"I keep track of people who interest me." She ground the beans from a canister and set the coffee to brew. The aroma mingled with the pleasant, herbaceous scent of the room. "You've worked with tribal police more than once."

"I have respect for the men and women who keep order on the rez. I hope to talk with them about a murder that took place last October."

Daisy remembered the victim found at the Riverwalk. "Is that killing related to these two autopsies?"

"I believe so," he said. "The victim was strangled."

"Eileen Findlay," Dr. Julia said. "I did the autopsy. Give my assistant her name, and she'll pull the files." She turned her dark-eyed gaze on Daisy. "Tell me how a biology teacher from Denver ends up in a graveyard outside a ghost town."

"Ever heard of Brighton's Bullion?"

"The golden treasure."

Not wanting to waste much time on the family myth, Daisy rushed through her explanation of why she'd been searching for the grave of the outlaw Sherwood Brighton. "We found the gravestone for his wife, Annie, at Butcher's Gulch. I don't know why this respectable woman was buried in an outlaws' cemetery, but she was."

"A mystery," Dr. Julia said. "I heard that you encourage your high school students to work with cadavers."

"I don't get to provide that experience as often as I'd like. Sometimes, there aren't bodies available. Sometimes, parents refuse permission." She was always surprised when the adults wouldn't allow their children to participate. "When studying anatomy, it's best to see a real-life example of how organs fit together—and work together—in the body. I also have botany classes where I make the students start a garden. I mean, how can they understand plants when they think all produce comes prepackaged from a grocery store?"

"You're a good teacher." Dr. Julia took both of her hands and held them, making a connection. "If you ever consider leaving Denver, there's a place for you here."

Stunned into silence, Daisy absorbed this special moment in time. The warmth of Dr. Julia's touch. The scent of earth from plants and coffee. The colors and patterns of the Ute designs. She glanced at Carter, realizing that he fit precisely into this picture, these feelings.

She cleared her throat. "Thank you."

"I mean it." Dr. Julia gave her hands a squeeze and returned to her coffee maker. She filled three ceramic mugs that bore stylized sunrise designs. "We have a strong community of scientists and artists. We can use someone with your skills. And your passion."

Daisy would love to work with this plainspoken woman who was also brilliant. "I read your paper on the advantages of the Rokitansky method in organ removal during autopsy, and I agree with your conclusion about how it's important to take your time."

"Even when you have a room full of officers who are anxious to hear results." She aimed a sidelong glance at Carter. "Those are your people, Ranger."

"I try not to be impatient," he said, "but you can always bluff me because I don't understand anatomy. If you told me it took a week to study the spleen, I wouldn't contradict. I don't even know where to find the spleen."

The doctor's laughter sounded as rich as her coffee tasted. Daisy's spirits lightened. "Maybe you can help me understand something. Scientific explanations make sense to me, and I can happily study forensics all day. But when it comes to speculation and deduction, I'm totally confused."

"Give me an example."

"When Carter talks about the investigation and starts posing theories. I imagine the serial killer as a predator—which, to tell the truth, he is. And I scare myself."

"You need solid facts to be grounded. I'm much the same. My brain works deductively. For example, I saw twin puncture marks on Rene's side below the rib cage.

My deduction—she had been incapacitated by a stun gun. That's a rational conclusion. Factual."

Daisy completely understood. She looked to Carter for his opinion. "What do you think about the puncture marks?"

"I'm wondering why he used it. When did he zap her—when he first captured her or right before he killed her? Did he use the gun on his other victims? There was no mention of puncture wounds in Hannah's autopsy report." He focused on Dr. Julia. "I'll be interested to hear about the victim from the reservation. Maybe Hannah was an outlier and he didn't stun her because he knew they were completely alone."

"So much speculation." Daisy sipped her coffee. "And no way of knowing the truth. I'm already imagining this monster terrorizing the women he killed. How can we ever know why?"

"Psychology and profiling." Carter looked to Dr. Julia. "I spoke to Joaquin Stanley."

"How is the old hippie?"

"Same as always."

On the drive down here, Carter had outlined his supervisor's profile of the murderer. They should look for an organized killer who was not sexually motivated. A stalker, he was fond of his victims and might develop an attachment to them. Probably, he was triggered by a traumatic event involving a woman he cared about, i.e., mother, sister, grandmother, friend.

After he ran down the same list with Dr. Julia, she gazed across the rim of her coffee mug at Daisy. "In my culture, there is a belief that the recently dead become ghostwalkers and stay close to the body for a period of

time. The killer might believe he is resurrecting a relationship that died."

She shuddered. Adding ghosts to her imagination
didn't help. She dragged them back to facts. "One of
our suspects admitted to stalking me. Should I worry?
Am I in danger?"

"Stalking might be a part of the serial killer's procedure," Dr. Julia said, "but there are others who stalk
for other reasons. Either way, it's a threatening behavior. That's a fact."

"Got it. I should take steps to protect myself from
this guy."

"We might learn more from studying victimology.
Again, based on fact. Killers are more likely to attack
when the victim is unprotected or in a dangerous place."

Daisy thought of Hannah being drawn to the memorial, where she'd be alone. Andrea had been grabbed
in a grocery store parking lot, where she was not alone
but surrounded by people who were distracted by their
own business. "What else?"

"Trust no one. Avoid risky behavior. And—this is
really important—align yourself with a suitable guard-
ian."

"Like Carter." She was still frightened but doubted
she'd be injured when he was with her. "No more visiting cemeteries by myself, especially after dark."

Dr. Julia asked, "Do you have any specific reason
to believe you might be targeted as the next victim?"

She shook her head. "Just my overactive imagination."

"There is something," Carter said. "We're examining
links between these women. Hannah was at the Riverwalk when the Ute woman was killed. Andrea was a

friend of Hannah's. Rene was close to the place where Andrea was dumped after she was murdered."

"I'm not part of those connections," Daisy said. "Maybe you should keep an eye on Pinkie and the other women at the party who were friends of Rene."

"Good idea," he said. "I'll mention it to the FBI."

Dr. Julia stood and drained her coffee mug. "Time for me to go back to work. Daisy, would you like to assist with the rest of the autopsy?"

"Absolutely."

She bounced to her feet as though her legs were on springs. Eager didn't begin to describe her enthusiasm. Without thinking she gave Carter a hug and a friendly kiss on the cheek. *Whoa, girl, that's not smart.* No matter how hard she tried to keep their relationship nonphysical, her natural impulses kept pushing her toward him.

Settling his cowboy hat on his head, he gazed at her from under the brim. His blue eyes shimmered. His lips curved in one of his sexy smiles while he informed her that he needed to check in at the FBI office and would return for her in an hour or so. "I might try to meet with Slade Franklin while we're in town."

She remembered the clean-cut, tall man from the party. Talking to him at Butcher's Gulch hadn't frightened her before. But now? When everybody was a suspect? It might be good for her to confront him again. "If you don't mind, I'd like to come along when you interview Slade."

He cocked his head to one side. "Why?"

"To face my fears."

"Shouldn't be a problem for you to come along." He

gave her arm a squeeze. "I'll be back. Don't go any-where else without me."

She watched the office door close behind him. For her, talking to a suspect—even someone who seemed as innocent as Slade—marked a step in the right di-rection. She'd treat this interview like a science exper-iment, separating facts from imagination. And she'd follow Dr. Julia's advice: find the verifiable truth and do everything possible to avoid risk.

Chapter Ten

After spending an hour and a half at FBI headquarters, Carter returned to pick up Daisy, who was waiting for him outside the autopsy suite. Bubbling over, she delighted in telling him every detail about the autopsy on their walk to his SUV, starting with how she and Dr. Julia had removed the organs from the body cavity, weighed them and prepared slides for further examination. According to their preliminary findings, Rene Williams had been a healthy young woman who should have lived a long life. As Daisy spoke those words, her voice quavered slightly, which might have been the first time he'd seen her show emotion about a dead person.

"It's difficult to imagine," she said, underlining this deviation from her usual detachment, "the loss of a young life. She'll never marry, never have children, never have a chance to fulfill her dreams. I wonder what she was studying in college."

He rested his hand on her shoulder, offering comfort. The cruelty, the injustice and the sorrow of every murder case he'd investigated—from his years as a cop in Denver to his career as a ranger—touched him. He'd given up trying to keep himself uninvolved and impersonal. When he thought of Rene, Andrea and Hannah, he experienced the loss and the pain. "The FBI contacted her parents. They live on a ranch in Wyoming."

"I can't imagine what this is like for them."

"Neither can I."

She paused outside the passenger door of his SUV and gazed up at him. "I haven't let you get a word in edgewise. What else is happening with the feds?"

"Forensics has a couple of clear footprints for size-thirteen shoes. The same size was found near Hannah's crime scene."

"Is that an unusual size?"

"Not really. I wear a twelve, and I'm six foot three."

"Anything else?" she asked.

"When you saw Andrea's body, you said it must have been covered or hidden so the predators wouldn't completely tear her apart. And you were correct. Forensics found scraps and fibers." He paused before revealing more. This fact might send her spiraling down the wrong path. But what was he going to do—lie to her? "The scraps come from white canvas, the kind of material that painters—or carpenters—use."

"A drop cloth?"

He knew what she was thinking. "Don't make too much of this. It's likely that Eric Wolff has drop cloths as part of his regular equipment. And Slade probably uses them when he applies finish on wood products."

"Drop cloths are inexpensive and common. I've bought them myself when I painted my kitchen." Her forehead crinkled in a frown. "Those scraps might point toward Eric, but the cloth doesn't count as a valid clue unless we find it and it's stained with blood."

"And that's just about everything I learned from the feds. Wiley was happy when I gave him a copy of Dr.

Julia's autopsy report for Eileen Findlay, the woman who was found at the Riverwalk. She grew up on the Southern Ute Reservation but lived in Pueblo, where she was a student at CSU. He's working on possible connections between her and Hannah."

"Other than Hannah stumbling over her body?"

"Yep." He pushed his hat off his forehead and tilted his face toward the sun. The warmth of early summer eased the chill from the autopsy suite. Outdoors, they were surrounded by life. Robins and wrens chirped from the trees. People rushed along the sidewalks. Afternoon sunlight glittered against his windshield. Though he and Daisy had already accomplished a lot today, it was only half past four. There was more to be done. "Before we go to the graveyards you want to explore, I'd like to pay a visit to Slade Franklin."

"The guy with the buzz cut who we met at Butcher's Gulch. The carpenter who might use drop cloths. Is he a suspect?"

"It's worth talking to him. He was one of the last people to see Rene alive, and he drives a camper truck that could be used to transport victims."

"Does he have a criminal record?"

"He's squeaky clean." Which made Agent Wiley think Slade was an unlikely suspect. Interviewing him ranked as low priority. "I called his cell phone, and he agreed to meet at his house in fifteen minutes. Lucky timing. He's not working today until he has an appointment to give a bid on a project at half past five."

"What kind of project?"

"Some kind of renovation." He opened the passenger-side door for her. "The way I figure, we have enough time to talk with him and drive to one of your cemeteries before nightfall."

He got behind the steering wheel and plugged the address into his GPS. Even though he was one hundred percent mountain man, he appreciated the convenience of cell phones and other technology. He glanced over at Daisy, who was nibbling on her lower lip. Holding back words?

She piped up. "Do you mind if I tell you more about the autopsy?"

His jaw clenched. He'd really heard enough, but this was important to her...and she was important to him. "I'm listening."

She tried to keep her explanation technical but he understood the whole disturbing picture. "While studying the brain, Dr. Julia discovered evidence of a concussion, probably caused by blunt-force trauma."

"Was she unconscious before he killed her?"

"I can't say with full accuracy, but probably."

"And so," he said, drawing his own conclusion, "the killer rendered her unconscious, either by blunt-force trauma or by zapping her with a stun gun. He really wanted to keep Rene from feeling pain."

She nodded. "Is that significant?"

"Could be." He thought of Joaquin's profile that presumed the serial killer had a fondness for his victims and tried to take care of them. If he was living out a twisted fantasy about a former loved one, he wouldn't want to hurt her...not even when he slashed her throat.

"When we're talking to Slade," she asked, "is there any sort of protocol? You know, like I could be the good cop and you could be the bad."

"Just be yourself." The idea of Daisy impersonating

any sort of officer amused him. Though she radiated a certain amount of authority as a teacher, she lacked aggression. "You're too well mannered to be a hardened cop."

In less than fifteen minutes, he parked at the curb outside a Craftsman-style house in an older neighborhood. Yellow with white trim, a second floor, a neatly mowed lawn and a clump of juniper bushes beside the detached garage, the house didn't look like the home of a thirtysomething single man. Too tidy. The chairs on the front porch were old lady rockers with flower-patterned cushions instead of sturdy Adirondacks where a guy could sprawl and have a beer. Slade's truck with the camper on the back was parked in the driveway.

That vehicle was one of the main reasons Carter wanted another interview. An important piece of the serial killer's MO involved driving from place to place, transporting his victims. If Carter discovered sufficient reason to suspect Slade, he'd get a warrant for the FBI forensic team to process the truck camper, looking for blood, fibers and DNA.

As he and Daisy strolled up the sidewalk to the front door, the screen door swung open and Slade stepped out. "Nice to see you, sir. And you, too, ma'am."

Though he was thirty-one, two years older than Daisy, Slade came across as younger. Long-limbed and skinny, he looked like he hadn't filled out. Though he had the beginnings of wrinkles at the corners of his eyes and his mouth, his features seemed unformed. His clothes—a short-sleeved cotton shirt tucked into beige chinos—looked totally inoffensive.

After Daisy shook his hand, she asked, "What kind of carpentry do you do?"

"I like renovations, fixing up run-down houses." He ran his hand across his brown buzz cut. "I really like tearing out old stuff. Demolition can be pretty dang cool."

Not a guy who used profanity, especially not in front of a lady. Carter suspected he'd been well trained. A stern mother? "We have a couple of follow-up questions. May we come inside?"

"Just one thing." Slade lowered his voice. "I'd appreciate it if you didn't mention that me and Rene spent time alone together."

"Why not?"

"My girlfriend is in the kitchen, and she gets jealous."

A girlfriend? Mentally, Carter moved him several rungs lower on the suspect list. Typically, serial killers weren't able to maintain relationships. "What's her name?"

"Brandi Thoreau."

"How long have you dated?"

"Off and on for a couple of years."

"Wait a minute," Daisy said. "I thought you broke up with her."

"I did." He winced. "Rene is the person who encouraged me to get back together with Brandi. She understood what love was all about, and I owe her for that. I'm sad that she died."

Carter wanted to correct this sugary remembrance to include the word *murder*, which was the most important detail about Rene's death. But the hangdog expression on Slade's face gave him pause. Carter empathized with the guy. Did Slade empathize? If so, that emotion represented another sign that he wasn't a serial killer.

In the living room, Carter settled into a patterned gray chair that matched the sofa and love seat. Not the furniture a young man would choose. Nor would he select the paint-by-numbers versions of landscape paintings. In the attached dining room, an upright piano stood by the inner wall and a breakfront displayed a collection of blue-and-white-patterned plates and bowls that could have belonged to Carter's prim and proper grandmother—one of the few adults in his family that he actually liked.

An unexpected fragrance tickled the inside of his nose. "What's that smell?"

Slade shrugged. "Some weed that grows wild in the backyard. Not marijuana, though."

"English lavender," Daisy said. "I have some growing in my yard in Denver. The fragrance reminds me of rosemary. It's native to Colorado. When you dry the stems, crumble them up and add a couple of essential oils, you have a great potpourri. Did you make this yourself?"

"Brandi did it," he said. "Come to think of it, Mama loves the smell. She puts the lavender into tiny, silky bags and tucks it into her dresser drawers."

"Sachets." Daisy perched at the edge of the love seat. If she was frightened, she wasn't showing any signs of nervousness. "You have a lovely home. Very cozy."

The swinging door to the kitchen opened, and a busty brunette in a sparkly, sleeveless tank top and skinny jeans charged through. She was a short woman in high heels. "Really?" she demanded. "Do you really think this old crap is lovely?"

Always polite, Daisy stood, faced the young lady and introduced herself. "You must be Brandi."

"That's right." Brandi shook her hand. "What do you really think about this ancient furniture? Those creepy old dishes?"

"Not my favorite style," Daisy said, "but a lot of people like the classics."

"Classic crap." Brandi rolled her big brown eyes and adjusted her long, bouncy ponytail. Her hair was an unusual reddish-brown like mahogany. "Slade's mama liked this cheesy junk. And he hasn't seen fit to get rid of it."

"Does his mother live here?"

"This was her house. He moved back home to take care of her after she had a stroke."

Slade stepped up beside her. Standing over six feet, he nearly matched Carter's height, and he towered over Brandi. "Mama loved her dishes and chairs."

"But Mama has been dead for two years." She planted her little fists on her hips and glared up at him. "Honey, it's time to let go."

Daisy shot Carter a glance, and he nodded. This circumstance—the recent death of a beloved mother—might trigger a serial killer.

"Okay, sweetheart." Slade smoothed her hair off her forehead. "Next week, we'll go shopping, and you can help me pick out dishes."

Carter introduced a different topic. "Let's talk about your work. You're an independent contractor, right?"

"There are builders and remodelers I work with a lot, but I'm my own boss." He sounded proud about the arrangement. "I like being able to plan my own schedule."

A telling comment if he was the serial killer. "Did you ever have a regular employer?"

"Before I moved back to Pueblo, I worked full-time

for a builder in Denver, and he taught me a lot. He also advised me to do an apprenticeship and join the union so I could earn top dollar. All I ever wanted to do was work with wood."

"Did your father teach you the basics?" Carter asked.

Slade scoffed. His voice took on an uncharacteristic bitterness. "He left when I was five years old. I haven't seen my old man ever since."

Carter was curious about the woman who raised him as a single mother but doubted he'd get an accurate picture from Slade, who cared so much about Mama that he couldn't get rid of her furniture. Or from Brandi, who probably hadn't liked the woman and resented the hold she still had on Slade. Might be useful to talk to a neighbor.

"My honey-boo is a really good carpenter." Brandi stroked the smooth parquet top of the coffee table in front of the sofa. "He did this, and it's gorgeous. I think he ought to open a store to sell custom furniture."

"Well, sweetheart, it sounds like you've got all kinds of plans for how I ought to spend my money."

"It's not like you're broke. Mama left you big bucks." Brandi glanced toward Daisy. "The old lady was rich. Not super-rich, but she had enough that she never needed to work."

"Don't make it sound like she was lazy." Once again, Slade's voice was bitter.

"Oh, I forgot. Mama was perfect."

Before the conversation turned into a spat, Daisy stepped in. "Brandi, my throat's dry. May I have a glass of water?"

"Sure thing." She pivoted on her extra-high heels. "Come with me to the kitchen."

Slade watched them go, and Carter watched Slade as his expression changed from a scowl to a grin. Totally appropriate if he was eyeballing his girlfriend. But he said, "Daisy is really something. Real ladylike. You'd better hang on to her."

"I intend to." *So back off.*

He exhaled a sigh. "I sure wish Brandi had spent more time with Mama. Some of her classy attitude might have rubbed off."

"Tell me about your mama. What was her name?"

"Elizabeth Hotchkiss Franklin. She never went by Lizzy or Beth. Always her full name. Elizabeth." He strolled over to a built-in bookshelf below the staircase and picked up a photograph, framed in simple gold. "She was a beauty, slender and graceful. And always well-dressed."

He held the eight-by-ten photo so Carter could see. The picture had been taken outside a wrought iron gate fitted with a weathered brass plaque for Rolling Hills Cemetery and showed a younger version of Slade in a dark suit and black necktie. His long arm wrapped around the shoulders of a dark-haired woman who almost matched his height.

"Doesn't she look great!" Slade said. "She made that dress herself."

Clean and stylish, they looked like they'd come from the funeral of an important person. Elizabeth wore an elegant, fitted black dress with long sleeves.

Tied around her throat was a silky scarf decorated with green and blue swirls.

IN THE KITCHEN, Daisy recognized more homey touches that had likely been passed down from Mama. The salt and pepper shakers on the drop-leaf wood table were a chicken and a rooster. Some of the tiles on the back-splash behind the sink showed a Dutch boy and girl kissing. The light wood cabinetry, however, was modern and beautifully made, probably more of Slade's work.

Brandi lifted a bottle from an array of liquors on a cabinet beside the fridge. She unscrewed the top. "Would you like a taste of something more interesting than water?"

"What is it?"

"White rum. Tastes like raisins."

Though she had no desire to get blitzed, Daisy figured one drink wouldn't make a difference, and the alcohol might loosen Brandi's tongue. "Yes, please. On the rocks."

"Slade tells me you're a schoolteacher." She scooped ice from the fridge into two short, clear glasses and splashed in a healthy dose of clear rum. "I used to think I wanted to do that."

"What changed your mind?"

"School bored the pants off me." Brandi handed a glass to Daisy. "And I figured I could make more money as an online influencer. I do vlogs—that's a blog but mostly video—and podcasts about makeup and clothes and shopping."

Her occupation explained the sparkly top—an outfit too fancy for loafing around the house. "You must know a lot about computers."

"Abso-flipping-lutely." She clinked her glass against Daisy's, took a healthy sip and tossed her head, sending ripples through her mahogany-brown ponytail. "So, Miss Schoolteacher, are you going to tell me why you

and your boyfriend—who is majorly cute, by the way—
are here talking to Slade?"

"Just putting together more details for the investigation."

"Nope, I'm not buying that." Brandi took another
slug. "Is Slade a suspect? Should I hire a lawyer for
him?"

"Do you think he needs one?"

"Hmm." Again, she rolled her eyes, which must be her
go-to expression. "Do I think my sweetie pie boyfriend
is a serial killer? No way in hell. Why are you here?"

Daisy took a ladylike sip of rum. Not her favorite
drink, but she didn't mind the astringent burn as the
liquid coursed down her gullet and splashed into her
empty stomach. She hadn't eaten since they arrived in
Pueblo, except for an energy bar Dr. Julia had given
her. "If Slade was seriously under suspicion, do you
think the FBI would send me and Ranger Carter to
talk with him?"

"Never thought of that." She drained her glass and
gave herself a refill. "You two aren't high-ranking inter-
rogators. Not to be insulting, but the feds would know
better than to have a schoolmarm chasing Ted Bundy.
Am I right?"

"You are."

"But maybe you're undercover FBI. That would be
so cool."

"But not true," Daisy said emphatically. "Things are
usually exactly as they seem. For example, your boyfriend doesn't fit the profile. Serial killers don't usually
have girlfriends."

"But he's weird about Mama," she admitted. "That's
a serial killer thing, right?"

"Could be."

"I'm so totally glad the old lady was so much taller than me."

Daisy finished off her rum. "Why?"

"Slade keeps trying to get me to dress up in her clothes, which are huge on me. And he wants me to fix my hair like hers. You know, that big '80s style. You can bet I told him no."

Before Daisy could say no, Brandi refilled her glass. More rum actually sounded like a good idea, but she set the glass down on the countertop. "I shouldn't have more. I haven't eaten."

"Come on. Drink up." Brandi smirked. "What can you tell me about the dead girl Slade was talking to? Do you think they did more than talk? Was she prettier than me?"

"Rene Williams was short, brunette and healthy. I don't think she and Slade did anything more than talk. She'd just broken up with her live-in boyfriend." Daisy wondered if the feds had interrogated Josh Santana. "Is Slade the kind of guy who plays around?"

"He seems shy, but I'm not so sure."

Daisy sipped her rum. "Does he often take off on trips by himself?"

"No more than any other guy. He goes hunting and fishing." Her gaze sharpened as she confronted Daisy, then she slipped back into her vlogging personality and rolled her eyes. "You can't possibly think he's killing off women in his spare time."

When Daisy shook her head, she could feel her brain rattling inside her skull—an effect of the liquor. "This serial killer likes to stalk his prey."

"Damn, that's creepy. And it's not Slade. My honey-boo is a lot of things, but subtle isn't one of them."

Daisy wondered if she'd said too much. She lacked the finesse to direct this conversation with Brandi. "Are you playing me?"

"That's how I earn a living. I influence plain girls, make them think that if they use a certain brand of mascara, their eyes will shine. If they use my lipstick, their thin lips will look full and lush like mine."

"You lie to them."

"And I get paid for it." She preened. "Listen to me, sugar buns. You're wasting your time talking to my boo."

Daisy felt the same way. She liked Slade. But didn't the people who met Ted Bundy say the same thing about him? *Such a nice young man.*

Chapter Eleven

Still staring at the photo, Carter listened to Slade's mono-
log about Mama, who was obviously the love of his life.
She came from Philly, where her family owned several
clothing stores. They'd made sure Elizabeth was well
provided for, financing her lifestyle with a trust fund.

Her son thought she'd been happy and had fallen in
love with the West. After his dad deserted them, Elizabeth refused to go back east. She got involved with
several charities in Pueblo, supported the ballet and
the art museum.

"She was a wonderful person." Slade's eyes gleamed
with unshed tears.

"Never remarried?"

"She said I was the only man she needed in her life.
Sweet, huh?"

"Yeah. Sweet." But Carter couldn't help cringing. It
sounded like Mama had developed a fairly unhealthy
relationship with her young son.

"She promised she'd never leave me and made me
say the same words back to her."

A very unhealthy relationship. "Does Brandi remind
you of her?"

"Heck, yes. They're both opinionated ladies. And they don't mind telling me what to do."

He often spoke of his mother in the present tense. Carter had a feeling that no other woman would ever measure up to Mama. Time to change the topic. "I have a couple of questions about your work schedule, starting with location. Do you always work in Pueblo?"

"No, sir, I go all over the state. Mostly in southwestern Colorado."

"Have you ever worked in Glenwood Springs?" Carter held his breath. If Slade has been in Glenwood on June 10, when Hannah was killed, he'd jump to the top of the suspect list. "Maybe earlier this month?"

"Not in June. Last time I was there, it had just snowed. I think it was April."

"Do you keep a record of your jobs?"

"You bet I do. Come with me to my office, and we can check it out."

In the dining room, Slade paused to play opening from "Moonlight Sonata" on the upright piano—a haunting melody that stuck with Carter as he followed the man into a hallway that bisected the house. At the end closest to the street was a bedroom. Carter took a backward step to glimpse the nondescript furniture with double beds and blah curtains. Probably a guest room. Next to that was a bathroom, which had obviously been renovated, probably enlarged. The cabinetry and fixtures were beautiful and new, reinforcing Brandi's opinion that Slade had talent.

The home office featured a custom-made oak desk and bookshelves. Across one wall were three-drawer wood file cabinets. Though a computer sat on the desktop, Slade lowered himself into the swivel chair behind the desk, reached into the center drawer and pulled out a ledger. "What did you need to know?" he asked.

"You're very organized."

"Anything worth doing is worth doing well. That's what Mama always says."

His mother might have died two years ago, but Slade hadn't buried her. "I'm surprised you don't use the computer."

"I most certainly do," he said. "It's great for running invoices and keeping track of payments. And I've also got mailing lists. But I like to use the ledger for scheduling. I can scribble in changes or switch things up with sticky notes. The first contractor I worked for used a system like this, and I adopted it for myself."

Carter suspected Slade was a good businessman—likable, skilled and efficient. "Tell me the last time you were in Glenwood Springs. And can I see your schedule for earlier this month?"

"Sure thing."

Carter came around the desk to look over his shoulder. Entries in the ledger were neatly numbered and noted in dark blue pen. From April 21 to April 25, he had installed bookshelves and cabinets in an office and playroom in Glenwood. There were other out-of-town jobs to Durango, near the Southern Ute Reservation, and at a hunting lodge in Buena Vista. Nothing special had been noted for June 10, when he was in Pueblo for an extended period of time working for a contractor on a development of five new homes.

"When you do the out-of-town jobs," Carter asked, "do you stay in your camper truck?"

"Sometimes, and sometimes I get a motel room. Depends on how tired I am and how cold it is. I've got my camper fixed up real nice with a propane stove and lantern but no extra heat."

"Must be comfortable. You took it to Butcher's Gulch for a mini-vacation."

"I have a platform on one side for a mattress. Underneath are cabinets for my tools."

"What about water?"

"I try to camp near a lake or creek." He closed his ledger. "I've been thinking about buying a trailer or an RV."

"What's stopping you?"

"Brandi would hate that. She doesn't like sleeping outdoors, and don't get me started on how long it takes for her to put on makeup—"

Carter didn't have to wait long for the inevitable comparison. Slade filled in the blank. "—just like Mama."

From outside the office, a burst of feminine laughter erupted. Brandi and Daisy stumbled through the door. Daisy's cheeks flushed a bright red, and he was pretty sure that they hadn't been drinking water in the kitchen. Turning to Brandi, she held her forefinger across her lips in a gesture meant to convey secrecy.

But Brandi wouldn't be stopped. She held up her slender wrist and pointed to an oversize watch. "You've got to go, Slade, if you don't want to be late for your, um, appointment."

He glanced at Carter. "She's right. Are we done here?"

Before he linked arms with Daisy, Carter pulled a business card from his pocket. "I appreciate your time. Give me a call before you leave town." *Or decide to kill again.*